The Professor's Secret

Peggy Bird

CRIMSON ROMANCE

F+W Media, Inc.

Published by
Crimson Romance
an imprint of F+W Media, Inc.
10151 Carver Road, Suite 200
Blue Ash, OH 45242. U.S.A.
www.crimsonromance.com
ISBN 10: 1-4405-9503-8
ISBN 13: 978-1-4405-9503-5
eISBN 10: 1-4405-9501-1
eISBN 13: 978-1-4405-9501-1

For Charlotte

Chapter 1

Had she been the woman she was pretending to be, Claudia would walk up to the man who'd just strolled into the waiting area at the gate, smile seductively, and say, "Let's blow this popsicle stand." He was so attractive, paying for a drink, a meal, or a trip to wherever he wanted to go would be worth it to have the chance to get to know him.

Tall and self-assured looking, he wore a tight, black T-shirt that hinted at ripped abs, a leather bomber jacket that emphasized his shoulders, and jeans that caressed a butt that every woman in the place was surely itching to pat. And then there was his rugged, fashionably stubbled face, sapphire blue eyes, and dark, almost black, slightly shaggy hair, which begged to be ruffled.

If she had the nerve to approach him, Claudia was sure she'd get a response. What she was wearing guaranteed that. Hooker heels, a blouse that barely covered her midriff, and a miniskirt so tight and short she suspected her gynecologist wouldn't need her in stirrups to do an exam. If it had been a Halloween costume, it would have been labeled "Slutty Romance Writer"—which was exactly the look she was going for. Today she was April Mayes, Queen of Steam, her hot, romance-novel-writing alter ego. She was on her way to her first big romance writers' conference and had dressed for the part.

But no matter what her outside looked like at the moment, inside she was still Claudia Manchester, PhD, professor of English literature at Portland State University. In her usual twinsets and midcalf skirts, Claudia was anonymous in any crowd. Not so now. People were staring.

Which brought her back to Mr. Hot and Handsome. Like several of the other men in the waiting area, who looked like they wouldn't kick her out of bed for eating crackers, as her grandmother used to say, he was surreptitiously watching her. But she was still too much the PhD professor to walk over to him and introduce herself, even though that was what April would have done. Maybe. Probably.

Oh, hell, what did she know? No matter how many times she reminded herself she was April Mayes now, not Claudia Manchester, she had no idea what she was doing. She had no experience as the flamboyant seductress her alter ego was reputed to be. It was a skill set she had never developed, only written about in books. Not once in the years she'd been writing had she imagined she would want to put into practice in the real world what her heroines did in their fictional ones.

She sighed and looked down at her iPad. Maybe by the time she got to San Francisco, she'd have gathered up her courage, and there'd be another hot guy she could experiment on.

Her agent, Mary Lynn Elliot, called what she was wearing "hiding in plain sight." People would look at her and wonder who she was but never figure it out. Claudia was adamant about keeping her identity as a romance writer secret, at least for now. If—no, *when*—she got tenure at PSU, she'd come out into the light, so to speak. Maybe. Although, as she tugged at her skirt to make sure it covered her private parts, it seemed possible a great deal of her was already "out."

Mary Lynn had orchestrated this makeover in Seattle, where she lived, not Portland, where Claudia lived, to avoid anyone who might recognize the professor. It had made sense. There was always the long-shot chance she'd run into a former student who was particularly observant or a colleague who knew her well. Happily, so far, neither of those circumstances had presented itself. The only people who seemed to have noticed her were men who were more interested in her boobs and her legs than in her face, much less her brain.

In spite of her inexperience as a blatant seductress—or maybe because of it—it was an oddly pleasant sensation to be the woman men paid attention to. It hadn't happened much in her thirty-seven years. Oh, she'd had her share of compliments and boyfriends. But she'd never been the center of attention she was at the moment, and she rather liked it.

However, the game plan she and Mary Lynn had worked out for this trip didn't include flirting with some random guy. It did include the wardrobe, cosmetic augmentations of blood-red talons where her fingernails used to be, henna-enhanced extensions to her chin-length chestnut hair, and a strategy for getting her on the plane without revealing her real identity. Flying from Seattle to San Francisco meant she had to use her real name—the one on her driver's license, not her pen name. She'd checked in curbside to avoid people who might be on the way to the same conference, just in case they were to catch a glimpse of her ID or hear a ticket agent use her real name. At the next hurdle, the TSA security gate, she was so nervous, she was sure she'd be pulled out of line for a pat down. She wasn't, and there, too, no one addressed her by name.

Now all she had to do was get past the gate agent without him saying, "Welcome aboard, Ms. Manchester," and she'd be home free. Her luck held. The man merely said, "Have a nice flight," before returning her boarding pass.

Settled in business class, Claudia watched everyone else stumble down the aisle, only too aware she was ensconced in a comfortable seat with actual legroom. It was hard not to pity the people sitting in coach. She'd been stuck in a middle seat on too many flights, feeling more like she was a cow being shipped off to a slaughterhouse than someone who'd actually paid for the privilege of being smooshed in between two strangers for too many hours. The urge to extend her sympathies was strong.

The urge to say something else arose when Mr. Hot and Handsome walked past and smiled at her. April Mayes would undoubtedly have paid the extra money to get him reseated next to her. Claudia Manchester pretended to fuss with her iPad. Again.

Besides, with him in the back of the plane, she could enjoy every second of the luxury she'd wangled from her publisher. A business class ticket, she'd argued, was a small price to pay for her agreement to participate on a panel discussing spicy romance at the Romancing the Writer conference. Mary Lynn, who'd had to make the pitch for the upgraded seat to the publisher, had reminded her this trip was not a personal favor she was doing but a long overdue fulfillment of a contract provision that she actively market her work. Claudia hadn't given in and, in the end, got her way.

Until now, Claudia had refused to even consider participation in conferences like the one she was now headed for. She wasn't afraid of public speaking by any means. She'd published, presented, and promoted work relating to her day job at professional conferences all across the country. And her lectures at PSU were known for being interesting as well as full of content. But she didn't want to be exposed to her colleagues, the ones who would be deciding on tenure for her, as the fraud she felt she was. While she taught Shakespeare, Dickens, and Austen, she read Roberts, Andre, and Gerard. Not only read them but wrote the same genre they did.

She would never admit it to anyone in the faculty lounge, particularly two specific old fogies in her department who she thought of as Statler and Waldorf, the two guys who sat in the balcony during the Muppets' TV show and criticized everything they saw. Her Statler and Waldorf thought commercial fiction was the work of the devil and the death of good writing. And they sat, not in the balcony, but on the tenure committee.

She didn't even trust her family with her secret. No thought stayed long in her mother's mind without coming out of her mouth, particularly when she'd had a drink or two. Claudia had learned the hard way not to trust her with any information she didn't want public—the humiliation of hearing about her middle school crush on a family friend from everyone she knew could still make her shudder.

Besides, her mother was too worried about the baby of the family—Claudia's alcoholic brother—to care about yet another of Claudia's accomplishments. No one except her late father had ever been proud of what she'd done with her talents.

Even if she'd been foolish enough to tell her, Claudia imagined her mother, like her colleagues and friends, would have found her career as a romance writer surprising. It had surprised her, come to that. She had devoured romance novels when she was in high school, but she'd stopped reading anything contemporary during college, sticking instead to the classic love stories by Jane Austen, the Brontë sisters, Tolstoy, and Hardy. Maybe because, as an English literature major, she'd had too much to do to justify reading for entertainment.

She also doubted that any of her past boyfriends and lovers would describe her as a romantic. She was too practical. Most of the relationships she'd had over the years were pleasant. Several were passionate but not of the hearts-and-flowers type of emotion. More the I-can't-keep-my-hands-off-you type. They'd all ended after the novelty had worn off or one of them had moved away.

It had always been just fine both with her and with the men she dated that it never got serious. They were as committed to their careers as she was to hers and understood that, while they were having fun, when it came down to it, work always won.

That's why it was unusual when, in the aftermath of a torrid summer love affair five years before, she'd written a steamy, sexy novel, using some of the details of the relationship and adapting one of Shakespeare's comedies as the plotline. She still wasn't sure why she'd written it. It just seemed to happen. One day she was working on a journal article about how heroines in literature had changed over the centuries, and the idea occurred to her to turn the Bard's work into a contemporary romance.

She'd finished it in a couple months and, on a whim, submitted it for publication. It found an agent, a publisher, and an audience immediately. As did the next books she turned out on weekends, holidays, and over summer vacation, releasing two a year to good reviews, a few awards, and steadily increasing sales.

Certain her colleagues would never understand what she was writing, she had kept a low profile as an author, never doing book signings, never attending writers' conferences, and certainly never angling for press coverage when she had a new release. Her agent, who wanted her to do all those things, reminded her about the Columbia University professor who had claimed her "other" life as a mystery writer, and the well-known romance writer who was also a college professor. Claudia pointed out she was pretty sure neither woman had outed herself until after her department had awarded her tenure. She refused to budge on the subject.

And yet, here she was, on a plane to San Francisco.

What had made Mary Lynn adamant about *this* event was pressure from Claudia's publisher who was sure sales figures would go through the roof if only Claudia would do some promotion other than posting on Facebook and Twitter and keeping up her website. There wasn't exactly a threat not to contract her for any more books if she refused, but it didn't take too much imagination to wonder about a possible underlying message.

When her agent pointed out the two conferences she wanted her to attend took place in cities far enough away from Portland to be safe, that Claudia didn't have a full-time class schedule this summer, and that she was already months ahead in writing her next book, her fate was more or less sealed.

The San Francisco conference would get her toe in the water. If she discovered the water was fine, her agent had her booked for the Super Bowl of romance conferences, the huge Romance Writers of America annual event, this year in Denver.

As the flight attendant handed her a glass of champagne, she wondered if she'd been foolish not to have done this before. Enough bubbly, and she might get used to the life apparently led by the Queen of Steam.

. . .

The Westin St. Francis on Union Square was Claudia's favorite hotel in all of the Bay Area. Its graceful charm and long history in the city spoke to the traditionalist in her, and the convenient location for the sights and sounds of the city appealed to the other side of her, the one that enjoyed a little adventure.

The line to check in for the conference was shorter than the line to check in for her room so she approached the registration table first. "Hi, I'm one of the speakers for the conference."

The young woman behind the table said, "Welcome. What's your name?"

"Oh, right, it's ... ah ... Cl ... it's April Mayes." *Damn. I'd better get used to using this name.*

As soon as she gave her name, a middle-aged woman standing at the end of the long registration table came forward with all the speed of a gale force wind. She wore a long pink skirt, a flowered vest ballooning out behind her like a spinnaker, and at least three chiffon scarves, and she gushed as she approached.

"April Mayes? I've been waiting for you to arrive, but I didn't know who to look for. I couldn't find a photo of you anyplace. But I'm so happy to meet you." She steered April out of the line and into the middle of the lobby.

"I do hope another of your wonderful books is coming out soon. I'm a big fan. You have brought a level of literary excellence to our genre few others have." She clasped Claudia to her ample bosom. "Welcome to the Bay Area. We're honored to have you make your first conference appearance at our event."

Claudia disentangled herself from the woman's scarves and arms. "Thank you. I always appreciate hearing from a reader."

"Let me help you with your check in." She looked around for a moment as if trying to find something. "Oh, dear, I seem to have left your packet and suite key over at the registration table. I'll go get them so you don't have to wait in line." She began to leave.

"Ah ... sorry, I didn't catch your name," Claudia said.

"Silly me. I'm so thrilled at meeting you I didn't tell you! I'm Alma Price, the president of San Francisco Area Romance Writers of America."

Claudia shook her hand. "Nice to meet you. I hope I live up to your expectations."

Alma laughed. No, she tittered ... something Claudia hadn't known until this point anyone actually did. "Of course you will, my dear. You're April Mayes." And she was off to get the registration packet and room key.

While she waited, Claudia looked around, curious about who would be in her audience when she spoke. What she saw was an eclectic group—women in floaty skirts, a few more with flowing scarves like Alma, others in business attire and sensible pumps, many in jeans and knit tops or T-shirts. There were even a few white-haired, older women in comfortable pants and athletic shoes. Every age, style, and kind of woman seemed represented. What was missing was much evidence of testosterone. She didn't think there was anyone male in the whole place, other than the hotel staffers.

As she scanned the lobby, waiting for Alma's return, she began to feel she was being watched again. She looked around but didn't see anyone, familiar or otherwise, who seemed inordinately interested in her. *You're being paranoid.* No one was staring at her.

Alma returned with a goody bag full of paperbacks, bookmarks, and assorted promotional materials from other writers, a packet of registration information, and her room key. "I can show you to your room, if you'd like. I'm sure you'll want to freshen up before the opening reception tonight."

"Thank you. It's very kind of you, but you must have a million things to do and I'm familiar with the hotel. I'm sure I can find the room." She stuffed the registration materials into her messenger bag as she spoke.

"I confess I do have a few other speakers to look out for. So thank you. I'll look forward to introducing you to some of our members at the reception," Alma said.

"Actually, I'm not sure I'll be able to attend. My agent will be here later this afternoon, and we're meeting to discuss my next contract. I don't know what time our meeting is."

"Oh, please try to make the reception. We've all been looking forward to meeting you."

"I'll do my best."

Claudia made her escape to the elevator with a sigh of relief. All she had to do was remember to respond to "April Mayes," and she'd be fine. Oh, and avoid as many big events as she could where someone might catch on to her masquerade. Beginning with the welcome reception.

Chapter 2

Brad Davis couldn't believe his luck. The first person he noticed when he walked into the crowded lobby of the hotel where he was staying was the woman he'd seen in the airport in Seattle. She was standing across the room, looking like she was patiently waiting for someone or something. Hopefully, it was some*thing*, not some*one*. If ever he'd seen a woman he wanted to get to know, she was it.

But before he could get close enough to introduce himself, a young-ish looking woman approached him.

"Professor Davis?"

"Mr. Davis is fine. Or Brad, actually."

She put out her hand. "I'm Lucinda Pennington. I'm in charge of the Romancing the Writer conference. I've been waiting for you to arrive. You've already been checked into your suite, and I have your meeting packet here."

"How thoughtful. Thanks."

"We wanted you to know how much we appreciate your participation in our conference, and we're here to make sure you have a good experience."

Brad would be giving a speech he'd titled "Writing Historical Romance with No Duke in Sight." A history teacher at St. Mary's Academy, an all-girls' high school in Portland, he wrote novels as Davis Churchill, deciding to use a pen name at first because he wasn't sure how his colleagues would react to his off-duty activity. But his meticulous research and engaging style had won him fans both in and out of his profession. He was proud of his work and although he still wrote under his pen name, he didn't care that everyone knew what he did in his free time.

"I hope you'll be joining us at the 'Welcome to San Francisco' wine and cheese reception in a couple hours," Lucinda continued.

"It'll be in the Elizabethan room, and we'll be serving some of the best Napa Valley wines. And California cheeses, too. It'll be wonderful."

She was so enthusiastic giving her little canned speech he couldn't have said no even if he had wanted to.

"There's a map of all the meeting rooms in your packet," she said, leaning into him and pulling out the relevant piece of paper. "In case you're not familiar with the hotel."

"I'm not, so it'll be very helpful. And I'm looking forward to the reception. Some of the best wine and cheese in the country come from not too far away from here." He glanced at the schedule paper-clipped to the front of his folder. "I assume I can sit in on any of the sessions even if I haven't registered as a participant in the conference." He smiled at the young woman, knowing full well the effect it would have on her.

She blushed on cue. "Of course you can. All our speakers are considered registered for everything. We'd love to have you take part in whatever interests you."

"I like to scope out the room where I'll be speaking and maybe get an idea of who the audience is. Sitting in on some of the other sessions helps."

She looked up at him with huge brown eyes. "Is there anything else I can get for you? Anything at all."

Brad was accustomed to young women looking at him like that. He taught at an all-girls' high school, after all. He wasn't particularly vain, but he knew what he saw in the mirror every morning was attractive enough to make him a target for girlish crushes, especially since he was one of only a handful of men in an all-female environment where the hormone level must be off anyone's chart. Just ask his colleague in the history department who was wolf whistled at when he crossed the stage at the annual awards ceremony. But like his colleague who ignored the reception he got that day, Brad knew not to respond to the implication in the question he had just been asked.

"No, thanks. You've helped greatly already. I think I'd like to go to my room and read through the meeting materials before the reception."

She seemed disappointed. "Of course. I hope I'll see you later."

"Thanks again, Lucinda." He smiled and she perked up.

By the time he'd finished with his young admirer, the woman from the airport was gone. He'd have to find another chance to meet her. The odds were good she was part of the conference. Most of the people in the lobby wore nametags and carried the same registration packet as the one he was holding. His best bet was to stalk the conference sessions until he found her.

She intrigued him for several reasons. The first and most obvious one was she was beautiful. Her long reddish-brown hair, luscious lips, big brown eyes behind her glasses, and killer body were enough to interest most of the men who saw her. Brad was no exception.

The second reason was the more interesting one, however. She wore the sexy clothes as though they were a costume she wasn't completely comfortable wearing. She tugged at the skirt a bit too often for someone who habitually wore things so short; she kept adjusting the neckline of the blouse as if uneasy about the cleavage she was showing, and she walked more carefully in those stilettos than someone who wore them every day would.

And the rhinestone-encrusted cat-eye glasses—she didn't handle them like someone who needed them. In fact, he'd seen her reading on her iPad and looking at the departures board in the airport with them perched on top of her head.

She also didn't return his smiles or his long, lingering looks the way a woman dressed like that usually did. He certainly didn't assume every woman he saw would be interested in him, but he did know most women, particularly those who dressed for show, would at least be curious about his obvious attentiveness. This one paid more attention to her iPad than she did to his—or anyone else's—interest in her.

She was a mystery on several levels. And Brad loved mysteries. Before he left San Francisco, he wanted to solve her.

But first, he had to finish getting his presentation organized.

It wouldn't take long. He'd given the talk in various forms a couple times before. He was a popular speaker, partly, he was sure, because in a field of writing mostly populated by women, his sex made him unusual. Plus, he'd carved out a niche for himself with his stories set in various periods of Oregon history, not in regency England, as many, maybe even most, historicals were set. In addition, his work was accessible and appropriate for everyone, including his students, because the "romance" part of his writing was largely in the mind of the reader. He implied, rather than made overt, what was going on between the hero and heroine.

Brad had nothing against lust and a hot night between cool sheets—in fact, he was an enthusiastic participant when the occasion presented itself. He didn't have a difficult time attracting female attention. Hell, he had a whole school full of giggling, teenage girls to confirm that. He'd even had several long relationships with some amazing women. Although none of them had turned into lifelong, happily-ever-after relationships, most had become warm friendships, some of which lasted longer than the romances had. But while sex was part of his life, he didn't feel the need to write about it.

Romancing the Writer might not be his first conference, but it was his first in San Francisco. He'd jumped at the chance when his agent had told him he'd been invited to speak. He loved the city and would never turn down a chance to stay in a classy hotel. Besides, his book *Mrs. Duniway's Assistant*, the story of a woman involved in the long, arduous struggle to obtain the vote for the women of Oregon and the man she convinces to help her, had recently won the Oregon Book Award for fiction, and the conference was a chance to promote it.

Now he had added the chance to unravel the mystery of a beautiful redhead in completely fake glasses. The next few days were shaping up to be everything a man could want.

• • •

"So, how was the trip down?" Claudia asked. She and her agent were settled in the Oak Room Restaurant waiting to order dinner.

"The usual. Too many people. Not enough legroom. But a couple vodka tonics helped."

Claudia laughed, knowing Mary Lynn had probably left more than half of each drink in its plastic glass. She usually did. It was one of her negotiating techniques to appear to consume a great deal of alcohol but not ever actually finish any of the drinks she ordered. "Who were you trying to bamboozle on the plane?"

"As luck would have it, I was seated next to Dane Black."

"Ah, the Lord of Darkness himself. Is he here for the conference, too?"

"He swore he wasn't, but what else would a literary agent be doing flying to SF and showing up at the hotel where a big romance conference is going on?"

"I didn't see his name in the program."

"Doesn't mean a thing. He probably isn't registered at all. He'll sit in the bar and wait to suck in whoever his target is, and before she knows it, she'll have signed a contract with him she'll grow to hate when he doesn't do a damn thing for her career but gets her novel placed with some second-rate publishing house that butchers her work but gives him his cut of the advance."

"Tell me how you really feel, Mary Lynn."

"Sorry. Didn't mean to run on. His way of doing business makes me angry. Which is a pity. He's damn handsome."

Her explanation of how she felt was interrupted by the arrival of their server. They ordered their dinners, which were brought out in what seemed like record time, and were finishing up when Tom Anthony, the executive editor from Claudia's publishing house, walked over to their table.

"Mind if I join you, Mary Lynn? Claudia ... sorry, April? And I love the new look, April. Mary Lynn did an excellent job of dressing you up as my Queen of Steam."

"Thanks, Tom. I'm still getting used to it, but it seems to be convincing people I am who I write as."

Anthony dropped into the chair opposite Claudia and ordered a drink. "I'm glad I ran into you, Mary Lynn," he said. "I was in a pitch session this afternoon with a promising young writer who has a book I think will be ready to submit soon. It could be either chick lit or romance. I gave her your name. She's going to need an agent if the whole book is as good as the sample chapters and synopsis I read. I asked for the full manuscript already."

"Always happy to get a new client. Thanks," Mary Lynn said. "And I'm glad you're here. I wanted to talk about April's future."

Claudia enjoyed listening to her agent arrange her life, so she was silent for most of the conversation that ensued as the other two people at the table discussed the details of her next contract. She knew she'd have a chance to give her opinion later, when she was alone with Mary Lynn, so she concentrated on her dessert, which was delicious.

When the two of them got into a gossip session about people they knew in the business, her attention wandered, as did her gaze. To her surprise, over in the corner of the restaurant, at a table with a half dozen women was Mr. Hot and Handsome from the airport. He'd changed from his leather jacket and T-shirt to an Aran sweater and presumably some form of trousers, although because of the table, she couldn't see what kind. He had a glass of wine in front of him, which he didn't seem to be paying attention to. He was, however, paying attention to the women at the table. In turn, they smiled, laughed, lowered their eyes, and blushed. It was like watching a group of high school cheerleaders competing for the attention of the star quarterback.

"Sounds good, don't you think, April?" Mary Lynn asked.

"Ah ... sure. We'll talk it over and get back to you."

Mary Lynn frowned. "Okay, if that's what you want." She turned to Tom. "I guess we'll get back to you."

Tom stood and put his hand out. "Always good to do business with you, Mary Lynn, April. I'll look forward to hearing from you." They shook hands in turn, and he left.

Mary Lynn waited until he was out of earshot before saying, "What do you mean, we'll get back to him? I thought what he offered was great."

"I'm sorry. I thought you were still gossiping about the business. I wasn't paying attention. If you think it's good, run with it."

Mary Lynn looked around the restaurant. "What exactly was interesting enough to distract you from a discussion of your next contract?"

Claudia nodded toward the hunk in the Aran sweater. "That guy, the one at the corner table with all those women. I saw him in Seattle at the airport. You don't happen to know who he is, do you?"

Mary Lynn craned her neck to get a better view. "You mean Davis Churchill?"

"The historical romance writer? I've read about his books but haven't read any of them yet."

"I think that's who he is. I can go over and find out for sure if you'd like."

"God no. I don't want to be obvious."

Mary Lynn cocked her head and smiled. "I've never known you to stare at a strange man before. Want to share anything with me?"

"There's nothing to share, believe me. I noticed him in the airport, and then here he is. I had no idea he was another writer."

"I'd say you more than just noticed him. You're as close to drooling as I've ever seen you."

"I don't drool over men. He's attractive, that's all. In a sort of obvious way." Claudia dug around in her messenger bag for her wallet. "And now it's time to end this conversation and get out of here."

"Sure you don't want me to go over and ask him to join us?" Mary Lynn was grinning.

"Leave it. I only wanted to know who he was. I wasn't planning a wedding, for God's sake." She pulled out a credit card.

"Too bad. The two of you would have beautiful children, that's for sure." She waved off Claudia's credit card. "Dinner's on me. And don't argue about it. If you do, you'll draw attention to yourself, which, if I recall our past conversations on the subject, you don't want to do. Although you are quite possibly the only writer who has ever lived who doesn't want to be known."

"My work should speak for itself."

"It does. But your readers also want to know you."

Claudia stood. "You're right, we've had this discussion before. And like all the other times we've argued about it, you've yet to convince me." She glanced over at the corner table. The man looked up as she did and smiled. She quickly turned away. "I'm out of here." And she made her escape.

Chapter 3

The opening day of the conference was in full swing with ten to twelve breakout rooms going at all times plus one major event in the ballroom for breakfast and one for lunch. The subjects ranged from the how-tos of world building to what records to keep for the IRS, from the eternal question of whether to outline or fly by the seat of one's pants to how to write sex scenes from the male perspective to ... well, to just about anything a romance writer could want to know about the craft of writing and the nuts and bolts of the business side of being an author.

The breakfast panel had been a discussion among the representatives of the publishing houses present on what they were looking for in new manuscripts. Brad had skipped it. He had no intention of switching genres or publishers. Instead, he had a quick cup of coffee and a bagel after which he began his hunt for his mystery woman.

At least he now knew she was with the conference. He'd recognized the man she was sitting with at the restaurant last night as Tom Anthony—an editor with a big traditional publishing house. So she was either a writer or an agent. Which meant she'd be here for some, if not all, of the next three days. But every time Brad thought he had a chance to meet her, she vanished. He felt like a hunter chasing Bambi.

He spent the morning slipping into the back of several of the breakout rooms to scan the audience. He didn't find her.

Discouraged, he joined a table of other historical authors at lunch while they listened to romance writing legend Nora Roberts talk about her long and successful career. Brad had heard her speak before but always enjoyed listening to her because there was usually a line he could pick up from her speeches worth repeating to his students. His all-time favorite was "You can fix anything but a blank page," which resonated with him because it happened to be his approach to writing as well.

After lunch, the second panel organized by subgenre was scheduled. The morning panel had featured contemporary romance; the afternoon panel highlighted spicy, or erotic, romance. Historical romance, the panel on which he was included, was scheduled for the afternoon of the second day, following his lunch speech.

Wanting to see what the acoustics and lighting were like in the room where he'd be on the panel the next day, he decided to drop in on the afternoon discussion. Steamy romance wasn't his field of interest, but he wouldn't be listening to the speakers much anyway. As he stood in the back looking around, taking mental notes about the room, the meeting organizer he'd met the day before began to introduce the panel members.

The room was rather large, with a stage and auditorium-style seating for several hundred people. The place was packed, due to the subject, he assumed. It was a hot topic, thanks to *Fifty Shades of Grey* and the rapidly growing market for same-sex romances. In fact, the woman now being introduced wrote award winning male/male romance. He was almost finished scoping out the setup he'd be working with the next day when he saw who else was on the stage. In an instant, he forgot about lighting, audio, video, HVAC systems, and anything else he'd observed about the room.

Seated behind a long table, along with five other women, was Bambi. And she was as stunning as he remembered her.

The light hit her red hair in a way that made it seem to glow. She was wearing the phony cat-eye glasses, which did little but call attention to her big eyes—brown if he remembered correctly. Even from a distance and somewhat obscured by a table, her knockout body was obvious. Her legs, which were visible, showed no sign of a skirt, although he was sure she had one on. What he could see from the waist up was some kind of drapey blouse barely covering her assets, which were sexy as hell.

And on the table in front of her was a nameplate reading "April Mayes." His mystery woman finally had a name, one he recognized even if he didn't read steamy contemporary romances. No wonder she looked like sin walking.

His plan to slip out the back door as soon as he had finished his recon now abandoned, he settled into a seat in the last row and waited for her to speak. He had no idea what the other women said. He was too busy watching her. She was a much more considerate listener than he was. She paid attention to her colleagues, her body language supportive as she leaned on her arms on the table, her head nodding in agreement with certain points and her mouth smiling at amusing anecdotes.

When it was her turn to speak, her voice matched her looks— low pitched and soft, it hinted at sex and a trip to paradise. Or maybe that was wishful thinking combined with knowing what she wrote. Interestingly, the sensuous voice still had the ability to carry all the way to the back of the rather large room. He was impressed with her skill at public speaking. She must have been doing this for a long time.

When the six women had finished their formal remarks, the floor was opened to questions. If she'd impressed him with her presentation, her stage presence as she fielded questions with meaty, informative answers blew him away. She never looked or sounded like she thought the question inappropriate, repetitive, or off the subject, although a couple were all three. His favorite exchange, however, was the one she had with a man who was clearly skeptical about her skills.

The audience member led with, "So, you're saying you don't write porn. You're writing sensuous fiction for readers who are looking for a story with explicit sex. Okay. I guess I accept that. But what makes you an expert on the subject?"

"Thank you for listening closely enough to hear how I described my work," she began. "Not everyone does." Then when the laughter died down, she added, "I wouldn't say I'm an expert on the subject, but I am—"

He interrupted. "So you're saying you haven't done all the things you write about?"

"I didn't say that. I was trying to say—"

"Well, are you saying you *have* done all the things you write about?"

She paused for a moment. Brad thought he saw a small smile fight to make an appearance. Then, instead of answering directly, she said, "Let me ask *you* a question. Do you assume P. D. James, Elizabeth George, or Ngaio Marsh wrote from their experience murdering people? And before you answer, I'm willing to concede Jessica Fletcher knew a lot about murder from her habit of stumbling across a dead body every week for however many years she was on television. But she's a fictional mystery writer. I'm asking if you believe the real women who write mysteries are like her."

"Of course I don't," the man said. It was obvious he was annoyed with her.

"So, you give mystery writers credit for being creative and talented enough to write realistically about something they have not experienced, but you don't extend the same courtesy to romance writers?"

The questioner looked like he was about to reply when he shook his head, made a sound of disgust, and stalked to the rear of the room. Brad fought the impulse to say "Way to go, asshole" to him as he left.

Paying no attention to his departure, April continued, "The question the gentleman asked illustrates a problem I believe writers of all genre fiction, romance in particular, have. We don't get much respect within or outside the writing community for writing creatively or skillfully. We're assumed to be hacks, or worse—writers who can't make it in the world of literary fiction."

She stopped to take a drink of water. "Well, in my opinion, good writing is good writing, whatever the category. We shouldn't dismiss a book or an author because the work is shelved as 'romance,' 'mystery,' or 'science fiction' any more than we should embrace bad writing because it's labeled 'literary fiction.' And we shouldn't assume the writers of commercial fiction are any less talented or creative than the authors who write other kinds of fiction."

Brad was about to give her a standing ovation, but she wasn't finished yet.

"Every one of the authors presenting here at this conference has worked her tail off to make her book the best it can be. Like other authors of commercial fiction, we want to give our readers a place to escape to, a heroine they can admire, a hero they can sigh over, and a story to make them think. We want to give our readers a happily-ever-after, just like mystery writers want to reassure their readers good wins out over evil and sci-fi authors want to reassure their readers the aliens can't defeat the earthlings. And, if it's well written, as much of it is, we deserve the same respect the author of a mid-list literary fiction book gets."

Although what he really wanted to do was yell, "Go, April!" Brad stood and clapped, which brought the rest of the audience to its feet. She was not only sexy but Bambi ... ah ... April ... was smart. Now that he knew more about her, he was even more intent on getting to know her.

• • •

Claudia ... damn it, *April* ... was stunned by the reception she'd gotten for her emotional response to the idiot's question. Thanks to her experience with bizarre questions from her years of teaching, the man who clearly didn't have much respect for her work hadn't thrown her. She was quite pleased by what had come out when she started talking about the subject. It certainly wasn't something she'd prepared, but it was heartfelt. In fact, there may be a way to expand it and make a journal article or a presentation out of it. The subject could spark an interesting discussion with her colleagues at Portland State. Or form the basis for an article in a journal after she had tenure. As soon as she got back to her room, she'd write down what she remembered of her response so she could work on it. Maybe on the plane on her way home.

When the applause ended, the moderator thanked the panelists and declared the session over. Claudia and the other speakers gathered up their papers and prepared to leave. Before she did, she took one more look out into the audience to make sure there was no one she knew who might be waiting to speak to her. After spending much of her time at the conference looking around in halls, meeting rooms, bars, even ladies' rooms, to see if she recognized anyone and not seeing anyone familiar, she was beginning to believe she was going to carry off her masquerade.

This room appeared as safe as all the others had been, although, to be honest, there weren't many people left in the room. Most of them had already gone to get ready for the afternoon and evening activities. Only the man who had led the applause for her defense of commercial fiction was still there. With the audience in the dark and the stage lights on her, she hadn't been sure at first it was a man. But now she could see broad shoulders and a male stance, which confirmed his gender. Whoever he was, she appreciated his response to her words.

Seeing it was safe for her to leave the stage, she picked up her papers and her messenger bag and went out the side door to the auditorium.

• • •

What the hell? Brad had waited at the back of the room for April to leave through the door behind him only to watch her exit through the door at the side of the room. The door cut off his view of an ass he wouldn't mind holding as closely as the short skirt she wore did. But both the ass and the skirt were now absent from the room, and he was back to running after his skittish wildlife.

Hadn't she seen him? She must have. He was about the only person left in the auditorium. It didn't seem likely she was trying to avoid him. She didn't know him well enough to want to do that. What did he have to do to get her to stand still long enough to introduce himself?

However, now he knew her name. Which meant he had a much better shot at finding her. He was sure she'd be at the book signing beginning in two hours, and it was likely she'd be at the dinner that followed. She may have slipped through his fingers for now, but she couldn't escape him forever.

Chapter 4

An hour later, Brad was in the ballroom where the book signing was taking place. He was early for the event and armed with a way to corner Bambi, assuming he had one thing go his way. It did. Lucinda Pennington, the young woman who had greeted him when he'd first arrived, was in charge.

"Lucinda," he said, presenting her with his winningest smile. "Could I ask a favor of you?"

"If I can do it for you, I will," she said, grinning up at him.

"Can I switch my table around so I'm next to April Mayes? I've never met her, but we're from the same part of the country. I'm from Portland, and she's from Seattle. I'd like to have a chance to talk to her about ..." *Oh, hell, what would we have in common to talk about?* "About her interest in ..." *Come on, Davis, think of something.* "Well, maybe putting on a conference like this. You've done such a great job, I think it would be interesting to have something similar in the Northwest."

Lucinda was beaming by the time he finished his stumbling explanation of why he wanted to be next to April. "Oh, I'm so glad you're enjoying yourself. It makes all the work worthwhile."

"Yeah, I imagine putting on something like this for a crowd this size is time-consuming. I bet it cut into your writing time."

"Badly. Not to mention my social life." She looked hopefully at him as if to ask him to make up for her lack of a social life.

"I hope you've kept good notes. If we decide to try to imitate you, I'd like to be able to contact you for advice." He winked and gave her his panty-melting smile again.

She giggled. "Oh, Mr. Davis ..."

"Brad, please. Can you help me out?"

"Brad, then. I'd love to, but I can't move authors from one table to another. It might confuse the readers who depend on the map we give them. And with fifty authors here ..." She let her words trail off, looking very unhappy she couldn't comply with his request.

"Well, can you at least tell me where she'll be?"

"That I can do." She rifled through a thick notebook until she came to what appeared to be a seating chart. "Oh, wait. Actually, you and Ms. Mayes are already close together. In fact, the author who was assigned to the table in between you canceled at the last minute." She looked up from her notebook with a huge smile. "I can help you after all. We'll just make sure the unoccupied table's been removed, and you'll be able to chat with her between book sales." She motioned to him to follow her. "The tables are right over here."

Ten minutes later, Brad was arranging the display of his books on his table, which was now a couple feet closer to April's table, as was his chair, which he'd casually placed off center and at the end of the table closest to hers. All he had to do was wait for Bambi to come out from the woods and into the clearing.

•••

A phone call with her department head—who thought she was in California visiting relatives—about the upcoming fall schedule almost had Claudia late for the book signing. She bolted from the elevator and scurried down the corridor to the ballroom, knowing if she blew this, her agent would kill her. Mary Lynn had promised to get her table set up with the large banner in the back, and the pens, key chains, bookmarks, and candy she was handing out displayed attractively. She wasn't sure if Mary Lynn would be waiting for her, but she did know she had to be in her seat behind the table when the doors opened.

She showed her ID to the volunteer guarding the door, found the check-in desk, and asked for her table assignment. But when she saw the chart of the authors' tables, she shook her head at what she was reading. Davis Churchill was two tables away from her. Whether she liked it or not, she was about to meet him. And face the challenge of keeping up the pretense of being April Mayes for the three hours of the book signing next to a man who made her heart beat double time merely by smiling at her.

Unless ...

She glanced at the name on the ID badge of the woman who was in charge of the event before saying, "Ah ... Lucinda, could I ask a favor of you? A friend of mine is here, and I was wondering if I could change tables so I could sit near her? We haven't seen each other in a while, and it would be so nice to catch up."

"Oh, Ms. Mayes, I'd love to help you out, but we can't change tables. Everyone has a chart of where the authors will be, and it would really mess things up to move people around now. Besides, Mr. Davis wants to talk to you about organizing a conference like this one in the Northwest."

"Mr. Davis?"

"Davis Churchill. That's a pen name. His real name is Brad Davis. He asked to change his table so he could be next to you, but luckily, you were already assigned to the table near him."

Interesting. Mr. Hot and Handsome wanted to be close to her. Well, close to April Mayes. Her pulse spiked at the thought, then settled back into a normal rhythm. Of course he'd want to meet April Mayes. She wrote steamy romances. She dressed provocatively. What man wouldn't want to meet *that* woman? However, if he was attracted to April Mayes, he wouldn't be likely to give Claudia Manchester a second look.

"Thanks anyway. I guess I'll go see if my agent got my table set up."

"Oh, yes. She was here over an hour ago. Your table looks ... well, hot is the only way to describe it."

Hot indeed. Centered on the deep crimson banner on the wall behind the table was a blowup of one of her covers, featuring a woman, her head thrown back in obvious ecstasy, and the back of her lover's head as he nibbled, sucked, or otherwise played kissy-face with her neck. Emblazoned on it was the April Mayes tagline: *Classic love stories with a sensual twist.* Although it represented exactly what her stories were about, it still took her somewhat aback to see it so prominently displayed.

The table itself had been artfully arranged with a half dozen of her books in stands. At the front of the table, easily accessible to marauding readers, were baskets containing the freebies she was handing out, all with her name emblazoned on them. With any luck at all, everything on the table would soon be in the hands of the women who were waiting in the hall for the ballroom doors to be thrown open, and she would be a bit better known.

As she approached the table, the man from the airport rose from his chair, which was as close to her table as it could be and still be in his space. He was wearing the Aran knit sweater again with black trousers. Up close, his blue eyes were even more intense. And his shoulders more impressive. He must have played football at some time in his life. It would be nice to run her hands over those shoulders. Have him run his hands over her ...

Stop. She had to stop. It was really inappropriate to be thinking about his shoulders or any other part of his body.

He grinned at her, an expression that warmed parts of her she hadn't realized had been chilly, and held out his hand. "We meet at last. I was beginning to think we really were ships that pass in the night. I'm Brad Davis, or, as my sign says, Davis Churchill. Although if you want me to actually pay attention, you're better off calling me Brad."

She took his proffered hand, quickly withdrawing hers when she felt a tingle moving up her arm to her breast. The man had more sex appeal than any ten men she'd met put together. "I'm C.

"... April Mayes. Nice to meet you. I hear you want to talk to me about organizing a conference in Portland. I'm not sure I have the time ..."

"Don't worry. It was the only reason I could come up with to ask to have my table next to yours so I could meet you. Turned out, I didn't need an excuse. We were already assigned here. Fate, I'd say."

"That's a relief. The last thing I need right now is another project. Between work and my writing, I don't have a lot of spare time."

"I hear you." He pulled out the chair behind her table for her to sit. "From your hesitation when you introduced yourself, I gather you use a pen name, too."

"I do. What I write can be a bit explicit so I decided to hide behind a pen name."

"If I promise not to be judgmental about your work, will you tell me your real name? Or do I have to perform the seven labors of Hercules to earn the right to call you Claire or Clara or Clementine or ..."

It wasn't hard to see why she was so conflicted about this man. One part of her wanted to know him better. Wanted him to know her better. Another part of her was terrified that if it happened, she'd accidently out herself, which could have disastrous results for her career. He was obviously smart enough to see through her disguise. She had to stop him before he made more progress.

"No labors of Hercules, I promise. Maybe a little time, though. Is that an insult?"

"No insult as long as you'll join me for the conference dinner tonight. I've reached my limit of interest in yet another discussion about the state of the publishing business and have run out of ways to politely turn down eager young writers who need a mentor."

"I imagine you get that all the time, don't you? The requests for mentoring, I mean."

"You're changing the subject. But to answer your question, since I teach at a girls' high school, I am familiar with the situation, yes. Although I probably get more requests of that kind from my guest lectures at Portland State."

"Portland State University? I thought you were from Seattle." The words surely sounded strangled coming as they did from a throat constricted by sudden fear.

"No, I'm a born and bred Oregonian. Never have lived anyplace else. I teach history at St. Mary's Academy. No surprise given what I write." He cocked his head, a puzzled expression on his face. "Why did you ... oh, right. I boarded the plane in Seattle. I'd been in the Puget Sound for a few days sailing with old friends in the San Juans. It was easier to fly from there than to drive back home so I could leave from PDX."

Oh, shit. This is bad. Not only does he work two blocks away from me, but guest lecturing at PSU? The wash of acid gurgling up into her throat made her feel nauseated. But she had to ask the question. "You guest lecture in the history department at the university?"

"Sometimes. Mostly I do a session on research for writers for Dr. McNulty in the English Department."

Ann McNulty? My boss? Can it get any worse?

He went on, "But you're still avoiding my question. Will you have dinner with me?"

Now that she knew he was from Portland, that he knew her boss and taught sometimes at her university, he was even more dangerous than he'd been as Mr. Hot and Handsome. There was no way in hell they should have dinner together. More time with him would give him more opportunities to find out who she really was. No matter how attractive she found him or how sexy those shoulders, eyes, and hands were, it was risky. Maybe too risky.

She barely knew this man. Suppose he notched his bedpost with his conquests or bragged about the women he bedded? Maybe he viewed conquering the Queen of Steam as the ultimate prize. One word to the wrong person—her boss, for example—and it would be all over for her. She'd never get tenure. At any college or university in Portland. The city was a small town like that.

Fortunately, she had a ready excuse—at least for tonight. "I can't, I'm afraid. I'm having dinner with my agent and editor."

"The people I saw you with in the bar the other night?"

"Yes. And were those women I saw you with the eager young writers you referred to?" The acid in her stomach seemed to have spilled over into her attitude and tone of voice.

He laughed. "No, they were members of the organizing committee. I think they were amused at having a man on the program. It's one of the advantages I have of being one of the only males in a female world. I get lots of opportunities to be a token. I like it."

"You did seem to be enjoying it."

"Right now, I'm enjoying the tone in your voice that gives me hope you would have liked to have been one of them."

Her stunningly snide retort—at least she thought it would have been—was cut off by the sound of hundreds of readers surging into the ballroom as the doors opened and the signing began.

Claudia couldn't help notice the lines at Brad's table were long, and most of the women in the lines stayed for quite some time talking to him. He certainly knew how to relate to his readers. Not one of them left without at least one book, a smile from him, and some of the candy kisses he was handing out. She could only imagine how many of them would have preferred kisses of the nonconfectionary sort from the perfect cupid's bow mouth of the man who sat casually in his chair, inhabiting his space as if he owned it and was only too happy to bestow his favors on the women paying him court.

Not that she wasn't doing well. Once she tore herself away from watching him with his hordes of admirers, she found she also had a steady stream of readers to talk to. Most of them bought a book. All of them took something from the baskets of goodies. A number of them got into conversations with her about her work and how she dealt with the attitude about romances so prevalent in the literary community. She resurrected some of her answer to the obnoxious man from the afternoon session. It sparked a lot of discussion among the people at her table.

By the end of the three hours, Claudia was ready for a nap and an hour of silence but had to admit her agent had been correct. The contacts she'd made with her readers had been valuable. Not only had she sold almost all the books displayed on her table, but she'd expanded her newsletter mailing list by a couple hundred. Several people had asked her to do a Skype guest spot at their book club, and she'd agreed to think about it.

Surprisingly enough, she'd even had fun. It had been easier than she thought it would be to slip into the persona of April Mayes when a dozen readers were at her table telling her what a difference her books had made in their lives. One woman even swore she had gotten the courage to begin dating again because of one of Claudia's heroines. How could an author not love hearing such a happy story?

After he had packed up his table, Brad Davis joined her at hers. She was still gathering up her remaining books and swag. When she smiled, he returned it with one of his that, she swore, could have melted the plastic coverings on the tables. "Did you do as well as it looked from where I was sitting?" he asked.

"Not bad at all. How about you?"

"About as well as I usually do. I enjoy these things. Not everyone does."

"I'm afraid I'm one of those people, but you seem like a natural at it."

"Thanks." He touched her arm, and the tingle was there again. "Can we get back to the conversation we were having when we were so rudely interrupted by the people who came to buy our books? If you can't have dinner with me, how about a nightcap after dinner?"

"I have no idea what time I'll be back from dinner. We're going someplace outside the hotel. And you don't know what time the dinner here will be out."

"I imagine we'll both be back here by nine thirty or ten, don't you? Why don't we meet in the bar then?"

"I'm not sure." She was tempted. Maybe it was because she was a little high from playing April Mayes for three hours, but in spite of knowing it was risky, the desire to get to know this man was strong. Stronger than any attraction she'd ever felt before for anyone. But was it worth the consequences she feared?

"Tell you what," he said, apparently resigned to her not responding, "I'll be in the bar until ten thirty, looking hopefully at the door every time a redhead walks in, waiting for you. If you don't show up, I'll drink myself into oblivion before staggering to my cold and lonely bed where I'll pass out until the morning. Which will mean my presentation and lunchtime speech tomorrow will probably be disasters, and my career as a writer will be over. But don't let me influence you. Join me for a drink if you've got nothing better to do when you get back. And are feeling sorry for me being so alone in a sea of strangers."

By the time he'd finished his speech, Claudia was unable to keep a straight face. "So this is what it's like to cross swords with a writer. You're good."

"I'll only believe that if you show up tonight for a nightcap."

"I promise I'll do my best to meet you."

"I'll take it." He touched her face. "And I'll look forward to it."

For a moment, as he leaned closer to her and she felt his breath on her cheek, he appeared to be about to kiss her. But he merely tucked a strand of hair behind her ear, saying, "That's been driving me crazy for hours. It's the only curl out of place." He patted her cheek and sauntered away without a backward glance.

The warmth from his touch lingered on her face, and the sound of his baritone voice echoed in her ear.

What had she gotten into?

<h1 style="text-align:center">Chapter 5</h1>

The dinner wasn't bad for a conference meal, and Brad had been to enough of them to be a competent judge. For a change, the chicken wasn't rubber and the staff managed to get it to the table while it was still hot. The salad greens appeared to have been recently harvested, and the rolls were soft and, if not warm, at least room temperature. Brad had been seated at a table with the other speakers, which meant the conversation didn't revolve around his opinions on how to break into the business. Instead it was another discussion about the state of the publishing industry and how authors are getting screwed. Nothing new.

The after-dinner speaker, a rom-com screenwriter, had been funny. Which was also a pleasant change. He told wonderful stories about his experiences in Hollywood turning his and other people's books into movies. However, as amusing as he was, he seemed to drag on for hours. Brad looked at his phone to check the time so often, one of his fellow authors finally leaned over and whispered, "You got a hot date or something?"

He was tempted to say, "If I'm lucky." Instead, he laughed and shook his head. He did stop looking at the time.

Finally, the event was over and he was free. Sort of. A group of his dinner companions asked him to join them in the bar for an after-dinner drink. When he couldn't figure a way to get out of it and still wait there for Bambi ... ah ... April, he joined them. His attention glued to the door, he didn't add much to the conversation, which several people commented on. He brushed it off saying he didn't sleep well in a strange bed and continued his surveillance. But no hot redhead appeared.

His feelings about the lovely and elusive Bambi had been all over the map during the course of the day. She was obviously sexy. The way she presented herself was as hot as he imagined her books would be. On top of that, she was smart, if her presentation was any indication. When he'd heard her speak, he'd been impressed. She commanded the room, made an excellent case for their genre, and did it with a sense of humor. He wondered if her day job, whatever it was, had given her the experience to manage a room as she did. He was sorry he hadn't found out what she did when they were talking before the book signing.

On the other hand, as much as he agreed with her about not assuming that an author had to have had all the experiences he or she wrote about, he had to believe anyone who wrote explicitly sexual romance was likely not an untouched and blushing young virgin. But, in spite of her outer demeanor, she didn't seem very forward. Maybe she'd learned to tone it down. Her reputation as a steamy romance writer might scare men off. Not that she frightened him. More like challenged him, which meant he tried to be at the top of his game when he interacted with her.

If he ever got any further than public interactions, however, he would really have to make sure he used his best moves. He was now sorry he had never asked one of his bed partners what they were.

However, by ten o'clock, he began to face the fact he likely wouldn't have to sort out what his best moves were, in or out of bed. She wasn't there yet and probably wouldn't be showing up. With a sigh and an order for a second brandy, he gave up and tuned back in to the conversation.

• • •

Dinner at a hot new sushi place to celebrate her contract should have diverted her attention, but all Claudia could think about was the delicious man who had set her imagination on fire that afternoon. Although she hadn't decided whether she would meet him in the bar after dinner, she was having a hard time putting him out of her mind.

The thing was, she wanted to meet him. Wanted to see what it would be like to behave like one of her heroines. She'd actually written a scene in one of her books where her heroine met a man at a conference and began a torrid affair with him. Of course, it was fiction, so by the end of the book, they rode off into the sunset in his cute little convertible for their happily-ever-after. Claudia wasn't so foolish as to believe something similar would happen with Brad Davis. But still.

What if. That favorite phrase writers use to think up plot points kept coming to her. What if she had the nerve of the heroines she created? What if she fully and completely embraced the persona she was projecting? What if April Mayes took over the life of Claudia Manchester for the evening and did what she bloody well wanted to do? Took the chances Claudia had her heroines take. Walked into the bar with the explicit aim of doing Brad Davis. As thoroughly, completely, and exhaustively as any woman had ever done a man.

No, not possible. She could never do that. Granted, he had a kissable mouth. And he smelled good. Like a freshly laundered shirt overlaid with something subtly spicy. A freshly laundered shirt covering a body that looked amazing clothed but begged to be seen naked. And those eyes. They had never let her out of his sight in the airport, and she had caught them watching her at the book signing more times than she was comfortable admitting.

Claudia Manchester didn't do things like have a convention hookup. She dated perfectly appropriate men who she met through work and only landed in bed with a few of them and only after the appropriate number of dates. It was an insult to her dignity to even suggest otherwise. But she wasn't Claudia Manchester this week, was she? And April Mayes sure as hell would have grabbed him and dragged him off to her lair the first chance she had.

"Claudia? Are you all right?" Mary Lynn asked.

Her agent's question cut through her haze of lustful imaginings. "Sorry. Thinking about something I heard today. What were you saying?"

"I was asking if you wanted to go someplace for dessert or an after-dinner drink."

Claudia looked at her watch. It was a little after ten. If she left now, she could make it back to the hotel by ten thirty. "No. Thanks. In fact, if you don't mind, I think I'll head back to the hotel."

"Give me fifteen minutes, and I'll go with you," Mary Lynn said. "I just have to finish up one little piece of business with Tom."

Her agent's offer to accompany her, which was the last thing she wanted, was met with a surprisingly desperate look from Tom Anthony. "Do you have to go already?" he asked.

Claudia almost laughed. Perhaps the dinner hadn't actually been to discuss her contract after all. Maybe it had been to give Tom a chance to spend time with Mary Lynn. Was she seeing romance everywhere she looked because she was in the most romantic city on the West Coast and at a conference where all they talked about was romance? Or was it possible she hadn't seen what was in front of her all along? She decided the only thing to do was encourage the match. If it was to be, it would work. If it wasn't, it would flop.

Come to think of it, that might work with Brad, too.

"You stay," she said to her agent, brushing off what she was sure would be an objection. "I'll cab back and see you in the morning." She left before Mary Lynn could stop her and with the full approval of her editor.

But the conversation had taken more time than she wanted. As the cab pulled up to the hotel, she checked her watch again and saw it was 10:35. She was late. She threw money at the cabbie, sure from the grin on his face she'd overpaid him, and ran into the hotel as fast as she could given her sky-high heels. She was Cinderella in reverse—running to get back *to* the ball instead of away from it, hoping Prince Charming hadn't gotten tired of waiting.

Out of breath, she stopped in the doorway of the bar to regain some sense of control over her raging hormones and rapidly beating heart. While she tried to calm down, she scanned the room but saw no one she recognized. The conference participants were long gone, it seemed. All of the tables and booths seemed to be occupied by couples who had begun to move closer to each other, touching, hand-holding, making promises with their eyes the rest of their bodies would be redeeming in a short while.

Brad wasn't there. At least he wasn't anywhere obvious. She took two steps into the bar, trying to decide if she should turn around and head for her room or make a full inspection of each and every booth. She couldn't believe he hadn't waited.

• • •

At 10:35, Brad walked out of the bar. Alone. His colleagues had left him fifteen minutes earlier nursing the last of his second brandy and the tattered remains of his hope that April would show up. It was apparent she had decided not to. He'd been pretty sure she would be there. Although at the age of thirty-eight, he was experienced enough to be realistic about his instincts regarding women. Most of the time, he was right. But not always. It wasn't as if he thought this connection with a sexy woman would find him his mythical soul mate. He didn't believe in soul mates.

Truth be told, he was happy with his life the way it was. He had a great job with a decent salary. His writing brought him additional income so he could travel whenever and wherever he wanted. He owned a house in Southeast Portland and an almost-new Audi.

And he had a group of friends, both male and female, to hike, bike, and go to the theater with.

What he didn't have at the moment was anything like a romantic diversion. He didn't think it was his current dry spell that was spurring his intense interest in April Mayes—or whatever her real name was. But it could be. He did know he was fascinated by her and the mystery of who she really was. He'd Googled women's names beginning with *Cl* so he could try them out on her, if she ever showed up.

All he knew for sure was, he was consumed by curiosity about her because he was convinced she wasn't the henna-haired goddess she was pretending to be.

However, no matter how fascinated he was by the puzzle she presented, he had struck out in getting the chance to solve it. At least tonight.

The elevator arrived; he got in. But as he was about to punch the button for his floor, he saw something that made him lunge for the "door open" button. He missed. As the door began to close, he used a shoulder to stop it, grunting at the impact, knowing he'd probably have a bruise there in the morning.

But it was worth it. Across the lobby, standing in the doorway to the bar, was Bambi.

It was all he could do to keep from running to her, to reach her before she disappeared again. When he got to the entrance, she was standing in the middle of the bar looking around.

For him.

Walking up behind her, he put his hands on her waist, leaned in, and whispered, "Can I buy you a drink?"

Chapter 6

A shiver she couldn't hide confirmed her worst fear. This man was dangerous. Merely whispering in her ear, he gave her goose bumps and caused her nipples to perk up and hope something good was on the way.

"Oh, you startled me." She turned and took a step back. If he had been sexy in a leather jacket and jeans and hot in trousers and a sweater, he was completely swoon-worthy in a charcoal-gray suit, white shirt, and red paisley tie. She could barely get her tongue to form something intelligent. "You weren't here." *Nice work, Claudia. Great response.*

"When you weren't here by ten thirty, I gave up on your coming."

She swore he said the final word with a smirk.

"I apologize. I'm late. I know. My agent and editor kept talking and talking, and I couldn't get away."

"But it all turned out. You're here now." He looked around the room. "Looks like the place is full, except there." He indicated the bar. "How do you feel about sitting there?" When she nodded, he spun the bar seat around so she could sit and took the one next to her.

After they ordered drinks, she asked, "So, how was the convention dinner?"

He regaled her with bits of the dinner speaker's speech as well as a critique of the meal, his dinner companions, and what they'd talked about. It was difficult to resist being pulled into the web he was weaving with strands of sheer attractiveness, intelligent conversation, and similar opinions on the state of the publishing world.

By the time he'd finished his report, her wine and his coffee had appeared. After the bartender left, he asked, "That's my evening. How was yours?"

"Nothing worth talking about. Just the usual negotiations with my editor over my next contract and the book I still owe them."

"Got a new book coming out soon?"

"Supposedly not for six months, but he's trying to push the deadline up to meet his production schedule and I'm resisting I have other obligations than my contract with him."

"Yeah, I hate it when my publisher does something like that, especially any time during the school year when I'm slammed with classes, tests, or college recommendations."

"I know what you mean. Especially the end of term."

"So, you teach, too?"

Damn. He was too smart for her to be so careless. "Yes, I do."

"High school? UDub?"

Seattle? Why is he asking about Sea …? Oh, right. He thinks I live there because that's where he saw me board the airplane. "Neither, actually. I teach at Bellevue College. English lit." *She'd read someplace the secret to a good lie was to keep it as close to the truth as possible. Her job before she was hired by Portland State had been teaching English lit at Bellevue.*

He smiled and leaned across the table. "Okay, we have Let's Get Acquainted out of the way. Tell me about the mysterious *Cl*— Claudia? Clarice?"

She steeled herself not to react to hearing her real name and pasted on what had better be a convincing smile. "You're not going to give up, are you?"

"I have to know, to tell the truth, so I can stop calling you Bambi."

"Why would you call me a boy deer's name?"

"I thought Bambi was a she."

"How could he take his father's place as King of the Forest if he was a she?"

"And now I know better than to tangle with a lit professor."

"Let's get back to why you called me Bambi in the first place."

"You kept disappearing. Like you had gone back into the woods. I was beginning to feel like I was hunting Bambi." He waved off what she was about to say. "So, I've answered your question. Now you answer mine: What's the *Cl* name you're hiding—Clancy? Clarabell? Clemence? Clio? Cleopatra? Claudette?"

"What did you do, Google it?"

"Of course. Have I hit it?"

"Well, I can tell you it's not the queen of Egypt or the muse of history ..."

"So, not Cleopatra or Clio."

"Or a clown on an old kids' TV show."

"Thank God, not Clarabelle. How about what it *is* rather than what it *isn't*?"

"You've already said it, actually. This afternoon." Which one of the *Cl* names he'd guessed would she remember to answer to? In desperation she grabbed one. "It's ... it's Claire."

"Funny. You don't look like a Claire. Too tame." His grin was infectious. "So, is the last name real?"

"Yes. Sort of. It's Mayes ... uh, Mason.

He reached across the table, his hand extended. "Nice to meet you, Claire Mason."

She took his hand and shook it. But when she tried to withdraw hers, he switched the angle of his hand so he was holding hers, not shaking it. "Not yet. I like the feel of your hand in mine."

Her heartbeat sped up.

"I've wanted to do this since I saw you in the airport," he said, and raised her hand to his mouth. He kissed the palm then took the tip of her index finger in his mouth and sucked gently. She couldn't hide her sharp intake of breath that accompanied his action.

As he continued to gently caress her hand, she could feel the heat from his touch begin to creep up her arm. Nothing like that had ever happened to her before. Not from just the touch of a man's hand. It was electric. And it affected him, too. She could tell from the way his breathing had hitched and his eyes had darkened.

"You feel it, too, don't you?" he said. "This chemistry between us."

She swallowed the lump in her throat and tried to respond, but the words wouldn't come out. Instead of answering, she shook off his hand and picked up her wine glass. "I'd be a damn fool not to admit it," she eventually said.

"And I don't imagine you're any kind of fool at all."

"Well, I'm not sure how accurate that statement is, but, yes, of course I know there's chemistry. I may have been a liberal arts major, but I'm not totally unfamiliar with science."

"Or the attraction between a man and woman, if your books are any indication."

She laughed. "So, you think I've done everything I've written about, like the man who asked me a question this afternoon?"

"I didn't say that. But I do think someone as successful as you've been has to understand the emotion, whether you've had the experience or not." He picked up her hand again. "But I'm betting someone as beautiful as you are has more than a passing experience with passion."

"Out of curiosity, have you read any of my books?"

"You're changing the subject."

"No, I'm not. At least, not as effectively as you're avoiding the question."

"I have not. But I can promise you as soon as I get home, I plan to remedy the situation." He smiled. "Have you read mine?"

"I've been meaning to pick up your latest, about Abigail Scott Duniway. I read about it online someplace. Didn't it win a big award not too long ago?"

"The Oregon Book Award, yes. But why that one?"

"She's always been an interest of mine."

"Odd for a Washingtonian to know about her, isn't it?"

She had to be more careful. She was so caught up in his kissable mouth and his brilliant sapphire eyes and his delicious shoulders, she wasn't paying attention to what she was saying.

"I helped a colleague develop a class on feminism in the Northwest." *Which was true.* "Abigail figured prominently in her syllabus."

"I imagine. She was almost single-handedly responsible for the vote for women being defeated five times in Oregon before it was passed."

"All because she wanted to link women's suffrage with a ban on liquor." Claudia raised her glass of wine. "Here's to her success in one venture and her failure in another."

Brad reached for her free hand. "And here's to success for us."

"Yes, success." She heard the quiver in her voice as the warm, electric feeling reappeared in her hand and began to work its way up her arm. "Lots of books sold."

"Not what I meant but worth drinking to." He raised his coffee cup and took a sip.

Desperate to change the subject, she grabbed onto the first one she could think of. "Do you not drink alcohol?"

"I do. But I've already had my limit for the evening. Don't want to run the risk of having it mess things up."

"Oh, right. You have a panel presentation and a lunch speech to give tomorrow, don't you?"

"Are you deliberately misunderstanding everything I'm saying?" His smile was sinfully smug.

"Crossing word swords with another writer is a new experience for me. I'm enjoying it."

"I am, too. But I think there might be something else we'd enjoy." He signaled to the bartender who had been hovering for some time trying to get them to pay the check. It was almost midnight, and he wanted to close out his till. "I have a nice minibar in my room. Care to join me there for a nightcap?"

"I thought that's what this was."

"Then a nightcap for the nightcap." He waved off her attempt to take the bill, signed his name to the check, and slid off the barstool. Extending his hand to her, he said, "I'm on the eighth floor. Where are you?"

She took his hand and stood. "Same."

"Good. Then you won't have far to go when we say good night."

She swore she heard him add "Or good morning," as they walked hand in hand to the elevator.

Chapter 7

Brad wasn't sure how hard he should push. He didn't want to spook her. More than anything, after the day he'd had chasing then flirting with Bambi, he wanted to take her to bed, to see if sex was the way to unravel the puzzle of who she was under the phony costume she was wearing. Because the longer he talked to her, the more convinced he was that the makeup and glasses were part of a disguise of some kind. And he intended to find out what she was hiding.

He wasn't normally the kind of guy who looked for a conference hookup. Quite the opposite. As a single man teaching in a girls' high school, his reputation was something to be carefully protected. And the last thing he needed was someone reporting back to Portland about how he bedded available women as soon as he was out of town. But this woman wasn't like any other woman he'd ever met. She made him want to do things he'd normally shy away from.

She was very quiet as they waited for the elevator. He wasn't sure what it meant. She could be rethinking her decision to go with him. She could be trying to figure out a way to head for her own room when they got to the eighth floor. Or she could be doing what he was doing—overthinking the whole thing.

When he saw they were the only two on the elevator, he decided to vote for option number three and act on it. After the door closed but before he pushed the button for their floor, he said, "There's something I've wanted to do all evening. So if you don't mind, I'm going to do it now."

The look on her face said she knew exactly what he meant and she didn't object.

He backed her against the wall and, taking his time, caressed her face, enjoying the way she turned her cheek into the palm of his hand, sighing. Lifting her chin, he touched, just touched her mouth with his. The moan that vibrated through her mouth encouraged him to take it further.

Adjusting his mouth to take full possession of hers, he began to explore her lips with his tongue. Her body relaxed against his until he swore he could feel every inch of her softness molded to him. The smell of her perfume filled his senses. It was some kind of exotic smell, spicy, mysterious, and damn sexy. Like the woman who wore it.

His tongue urged her to part her lips. As she did, her arms circled his neck and the kiss intensified. Their tongues played hide and seek with each other. His hands slid down her back to her bottom and snugged her against his rapidly growing erection.

He was only a few seconds away from touching one of the lovely, full breasts teasing his chest when the elevator jerked to a start and began to rise.

Claire laughed against his mouth. "Did we do that?"

He moved a step back from her, regretting immediately the loss of contact with her body. "I certainly didn't. My hands were otherwise occupied."

"Mmm. Me, too. Must be someone else calling the elevator."

"Then we better try to behave." He punched the button for the eighth floor. "With luck, we'll get off before whoever called the car gets on."

Luck was with them. They got to their floor without a stop. As they walked down the hall, holding hands again, he said, "Still up for a nightcap?"

"Now more than ever."

•••

Claudia's breath hitched at the thought of what drew closer with every step away from the elevator—Brad Davis's bed. She was no reluctant virgin, but she'd never had a one-night stand. Never gone off to a strange man's room after closing down a bar. Never kissed a man in a public elevator. Apparently April Mayes ... ah ... Claire Mason or whoever the hell she was tonight ... did all those things and was in charge. Claudia was willingly going along with whichever of her convoluted alter egos she was channeling at the moment, not because she was curious but because of this man.

This unusual behavior was more than merely acting the part she'd been playing to go along with her disguise. More than trying to experience what the heroines she'd created had felt. The "more" was something she hadn't quite dissected yet. It involved the indefinable appeal Brad Davis projected. Ever since the airport, she'd been aware of him. He was smart, funny, and, God knows, sexy as hell. She loved talking to him—every conversation they'd had engaged both her mind and her heart. He was the perfect foil for her bad girl/April Mayes/sensual writer role. Whether he could be the same for her as Claudia Manchester remained to be seen. But she wasn't going to worry about that right now.

He stopped at room 810. "This is me." Swiping the keycard, he opened the door and stepped aside so she could enter. He flipped a switch, and the light over a small table near the window came on.

His room was neat and tidy, of course. The staff had straightened it all up and turned down his bed carefully. But his suitcase was open on top of the low chest opposite the bed with shirts and dark red boxer shorts spilling out of it. Two pairs of shoes were on the floor under the table. The tabletop was covered with papers, books, and a laptop computer.

He pulled open the door of the minibar and peered in. "I'm sticking to water. What can I get you?"

"Nothing thanks. I've had my limit tonight, too." Before she could sit, he was in front of her, taking her hands, pulling her toward him.

"Thank God. I'm finished with conversation, booze, and anything other than this." Before she could react, he had claimed her mouth in a blazing hot kiss that warmed up the room and melted away any second thoughts she might have had. Melted thoughts of any kind at all, actually.

He nibbled her mouth to end the kiss then nipped his way to her ear. He whispered, "I swear I could strip you and take you in five minutes, I'm so ready for this. But I don't want to hurry. I want to take my time so I can enjoy every single inch of you."

She sucked in a breath. "Why, yes. That sounds like a good idea."

He chuckled. "And you sound remarkably like a teacher talking to a slightly naughty pupil when she's not really sure she approves."

The shock of his blunt statement of what he wanted was now replaced by a determination to completely rid herself of Claudia Manchester, PhD for the night. She slid her hands down between them and unbuttoned his jacket. Saying, "Does it? Maybe you're feeling naughty and projecting." She pushed her hands up to his shoulders to remove his jacket. When it hit the ground, she started to work on his shirt.

"You might be right. I've never had a naughty teacher get me out of my clothes." As she reached the top button, he said, "Let me help," and yanked off his tie.

Because she'd forgotten about cuff buttons, she couldn't get the shirt off him. He grinned down at her and undid his cuffs, giving her the chance to admire the amazing set of abs she'd uncovered while he did. Her mouth went dry at the sight. She ran her hands up and down, through the valleys and over the hills of his chest and abdomen. He was more than in shape. He was perfect.

She must have made a noise because after he dropped his shirt on the floor and put his arms around her again, he said, "You're making an interesting sound. Can I take it you like what you see?"

"Oh, yeah. I like it very much. You're much better than anything I've seen in the faculty gym."

"It's my turn now," he said. He deftly pulled the zipper in the back of her little black dress down, and the dress seemed to somehow slip off and puddle on the floor. When the skimpy black lace bra she was wearing joined the dress, it was his turn to make interesting noises. "Jesus, woman. You are the most beautiful thing I've ever seen." He caressed a breast, ducked his head, and took a taste, a brief taste, of the nipple.

It wasn't enough for her. She wanted more. With shaking hands, she fumbled at the belt on his pants. He stopped her. "How about I get you settled over there." He gestured toward the bed. "And then I'll join you."

She nodded and walked on wobbly legs to the side of the bed. He turned her around and gently urged her to sit. When she had, he removed the glasses she was wearing then knelt and took off one of her shoes and began a slow, sensuous trail of kisses up her now shoeless leg. When he reached the barrier of her bikini panties, instead of removing them and continuing to the place she wanted him to kiss, he switched legs. She groaned as he retreated down her other leg. When he got to her foot, he removed the second shoe and then swung both legs up onto the bed.

Heat pooled in her sex. She was desperate for him to touch her, kiss her there. Now.

Instead, he went to the other side of the room where he removed his belt, shoes and socks, trousers, and boxers in what seemed like only seconds. Not long enough at any rate for her to appreciate the show of masculine perfection she was privy to. Before he joined her, he removed something from his suitcase.

When he sat down next to her, he put the "something" on her bed stand. A condom. He was prepared. Just like all her heroes were.

He bent to her and combed his fingers through her hair, drawing her head up to meet him. This time, the kiss started out with a hunger that had an almost desperate edge to it. But somewhere in the middle of it, he loosened his hold on her and turned the kiss into something softer, more subdued.

What had she done? Had he changed his mind? She was confused. He seemed to sense her anxiety. "I'm trying hard not to revel in the fact that you're in my bed, but after seeming to avoid me all day, I have to know the answer to this—why did you agree to come back to my room?"

His question startled her. "Do you always doubt the motives of the women who come to your room?"

"I don't ask women back to my hotel room. Ever. I guard my reputation like it was my livelihood, which it is. So your question is moot."

She licked her lips and saw the shadows in his eyes darken. "Okay. Then I'll answer your question if you answer one of mine."

"Deal. What do you want to know?"

"Why me? Why break your rule for me?"

"Easy answer. You're a mystery. I knew from the first time I saw you in the airport I wanted to find out more about you."

"I guess any man would who saw a woman dressed like I was."

"Yes, it was the way you were dressed that intrigued me but not the way you're thinking. You looked like you were wearing a costume. Like the clothes you had on weren't what you usually wore. You walked cautiously, like you didn't wear those stilettos every day. And you kept pulling at your skirt as though you thought it was too short."

"It was." She remembered only too well how uncomfortable the damn skirt had made her.

"Not from where I was sitting, it wasn't. There was one other thing. You don't need these." He picked up the glasses he'd taken from her a few minutes before, tried them on, and laughed. "Aha. As I thought. Clear glass."

It was getting too uncomfortable for her. He was chipping away at her April Mayes persona, getting way too close to what was underneath, and she didn't like it.

She reached for him. "We're sitting here—well, you're sitting, I'm lying down—naked, wasting a perfectly good bed, chatting about glasses and miniskirts. I thought you had some ideas about what you wanted to do when we got in bed."

He gestured for her to move over, and when she did, he joined her. "I definitely do. As soon as you answer my question. Why did you agree to be here?"

She drew his mouth to hers. The kiss tingled from her mouth to her chest through her belly down to her toes. It was better than anything she'd read or written because it was happening to her, not to a fictional character. From his reaction, it was as good for him as it was for her. Breathless, she broke from the kiss. "That's why. Did I give a good enough answer?"

He groaned. "The best."

For a few anxious moments, she'd been afraid he was more interested in unraveling the mystery of her glasses and her clothes than he was in delivering on his promise of what he planned to do with her body. But now he was back on track. At least, the track she was interested in. She was flat on her back with all of his gorgeous muscles pinning her to the mattress while his lips thoroughly and systematically took possession of her mouth, then her throat, and finally, thank you, God, her breasts.

His hands were magic, too. While one breast was being suckled and nibbled, the other was massaged, the nipple tweaked as if to prepare it for attention from his mouth. She was close to coming only from what he was doing to her mouth and her breasts.

She opened her legs to give him a space to cradle an impressive erection. As if they had a mind of their own, her hips canted up and rubbed against him. "Oh, God, Brad. That feels so good."

"You haven't begun to feel good yet, lovely."

He pushed himself up onto his elbows and began to trace a line of kisses from her breast to her navel then down to the now damp curls at the junction of her thighs. He breathed on her sex, and she thought she'd melt. When he licked open her lower lips, she did melt. Or at least she thought she had. His talented mouth licked and sucked and nibbled at her until she didn't think she could bear it any longer.

"Please, Brad. I need you inside me."

"Soon, lovely, soon. But first I want to watch you come like this."

After one more suck on her now sensitive clitoris, as if he had ordered her to do so, she flew apart. The universe contracted to only what he was doing to her as she saw stars and galaxies and felt her body give up every ounce of control.

It took a few moments for her to come back to earth again. When she opened her eyes, he was beside her, stroking her hair, his breathing as ragged and rapid as hers. "That was amazing," she said.

"Not as amazing as it's about to get." He reached over her and grabbed the condom. "Help me get this on."

• • •

He wasn't sure they were ever going to get the damn condom wrapper open. Both of them were fumbling with the thing, both still feeling the effects of the orgasm she'd had. He couldn't remember being so shaken by a partner's climax before, but when she'd arched her back and pulled at his hair as he tongued her clitoris, he swore he could feel the same orgasm rip through him.

When they finally got the condom on his erection, he rolled her under him, their legs tangling as she made room for his aching cock. Her hands were all over his back and shoulders as she pressed her body against him. He wanted the moment to last forever.

Wanted to memorize the image of her with a flushed face, her breath coming quickly, her eager hands roaming all over his body.

"You're so beautiful," he said, his voice tight with desire.

"Please, please, Brad." She was moving restlessly under him as she pleaded with him. "I want you. Now."

He entered her slowly, carefully, not wanting to hurry even though his body was telling him to bury himself in her as deep as he could. When she gasped, he stopped moving, afraid he had hurt her. "Claire? Are you okay?"

"Oh, God, please don't stop." She slid her hands down his back and squeezed his ass. He was sure he'd have fingernail marks there the next day. Marks he'd be happy to have, given how incredibly hot and tight and wet she was. And how happy his cock was inside her.

He started moving again, taking long, slow strokes, pulling almost all the way out then entering her again. Then again. And again. Their bodies moved easily, slipping and sliding on the sweat they were generating as well as the wetness of her sex.

"Harder. Please." She arched up, and he obliged, driving deeper than he thought possible. He wasn't sure he could tell where he ended and she began.

She began to whimper and angled her hips against him. He could feel her internal muscles begin to tighten. She called his name, and he lost all control. Surging into her, he yelled, "Claire" and he let go as his orgasm ripped through him.

Chapter 8

After their second round of sex, which was even better than the first one, Brad had dozed off, but his leg was still over Claudia's and his arm was across her chest. She lay there not sure what to do. She knew she should go back to her room. But she was sated—boneless, as romance writers inevitably described it—from the best sex she'd ever had. Never had making love been such a wild and satisfying experience. It was more like the sex she wrote about than the sex she'd actually experienced.

It must be Brad. The man was simply amazing. He knew more about what to do with his own body and hers than anyone she'd ever been with. From their first kiss, they'd clicked like lovers of long standing, not like two people who barely knew each other. Every part of their bodies had fit perfectly. Fit and functioned better than anything she'd experienced before.

Of course, she'd been different, too—wilder, freer, more passionate than ever before. Maybe inhabiting her April Mayes persona was something she should have done years ago if it gave her the chance to have the experience she'd had with Brad.

Her only regret was he had called out her fake name when he climaxed. Part of her had apparently held on to the hope he really could see through her disguise and would say "Claudia" at the right moment.

While she was sorting it out, she felt him stirring—all parts of him. Could he really be ready for round three?

"Mmm," he began as he nuzzled her neck. "If I'd known sex with a notorious romance writer would be so good, I might have tried to track one down and seduce her before tonight." He slid his hand up her rib cage, but before he could reach her breast, she caught it, brought it to her lips, and kissed it.

"Time for me to leave. I may be a notorious writer but I don't like gossip about my personal life. And I don't know who else is on this floor. There might be someone who's very interested in seeing me emerge from your room in the middle of the night."

He shook off her hand and returned to working his way up her body. "No one would be surprised, would they? Not if they've read anything you've written."

She inched her way back toward the side of the bed. "I thought you'd never read my work."

His hand continued its exploration as he laughed and said, "Oh, right. Busted. I've already confessed to that, haven't I?"

"So you're going on my reputation."

"Partly. Partly hearing the panel you were on this afternoon."

"I didn't see you there." She cocked her head. "Are you sure you're not trying to convince me to make love with you again by claiming you heard me?"

"I was the first person to applaud after you put that jerk in his place, although I was disappointed you left Agatha Christie, my personal favorite, off your list of women mystery writers who have probably never murdered anyone. I almost stood up and, instead of applauding, mentioned the name of one female mystery writer who actually had killed someone. Just to see if I could throw you off."

"Okay, you *were* there. And thank you for not bringing up Anne Perry." She ran her hands over his shoulders, suddenly remembering the man in the shadows in the last row. "Were you in the back of the room, by any chance?"

"Yup. I waited for you to finish up so I could introduce myself to you, but you ran out the side door before I could grab you. I had to wait until the book signing to get you to stand still."

Continuing to caress his shoulders, she said, "Ah, yes. I thought I recognized these. I couldn't really see your face, only the outline of your body. But your gorgeous shoulders give you away. You must have played football in high school or college."

"Football in high school; rugby in college. Happy they got put to good use by attracting your attention." He started kissing his way up her arm. "Sure I can't convince you to stay for a while?"

"Positive."

"Then tell me when we can see each other again. Even if we live at opposite ends of I-5, surely we can figure it out."

Of course. He thinks I live in Seattle. "Or maybe we can write this off as a convention hookup."

"Is that what this has been? Or is it what you want it to be?"

He sounded worried, which made her happy for some reason she'd think about later. "I don't think so. But can I think about it? I've never been good at long-distance relationships."

"Have you had a lot of experience with them?"

"Once. It didn't work out." How could she keep this up? It wouldn't really be long distance. All she had to do was walk a couple blocks, and she could trip over him. Which was the problem.

Before she could decide what to say next, he hopped out of bed, giving her the chance to admire, once again, the sculpted muscles of his body. Her attention distracted, she sighed with pleasure.

"That was a good sound. Does it mean you've thought about it long enough and want to meet me someplace after we're home?"

Damn. Discovered again. "I haven't decided yet, although I'm feeling pretty good right about now."

He was rummaging around in his messenger bag as he replied. "You want to flatter my ego a bit and tell me why?" A cocky grin appeared.

"I very much doubt your ego needs flattering. With the way you look," she nodded toward him, "teaching at a girls' school, I imagine you get more than enough ego inflation on a regular basis."

"As much as I appreciate your compliment, I would lose my job, and probably get arrested, if I wandered around St. Mary's like this."

The flush turning her face bright red, she hoped, was hidden in the dimly lit room. "You know I didn't mean to suggest you teach in the nude."

"Of course you didn't. But making you think I understood it that way made you blush in the nicest way." He pulled a business card out of his messenger bag and, returning to the bed, sat down on her side before handing it to her. "This is my card. It has my e-mail address and phone number on it. When you decide what you want to do, call me. I'll meet you anywhere, anytime."

• • •

An hour later, Claudia was tossing from side to side, plumping pillows, pulling up then throwing off blankets and comforters, unable to settle down to sleep. It was absurd. She needed to rest. She didn't have a speech the next day, but she was on a morning panel of *NYT* and *USA Today* best-selling authors responding to a keynote speech about the future of romance writing. She hadn't needed to prepare remarks. And she doubted it would be hard for her to respond. She'd read the speaker's article in the RWA magazine and was sure she knew what she'd be hearing.

Still, she needed to be sharp so she could continue to pull off her April Mayes masquerade, which meant looking fresh and rested.

At least until she got to the plane. Then she could relax, maybe even sleep. No one on her flight home would care if she looked tired. But her flight wasn't until the afternoon although she was sure Mary Lynn would want to skip the lunch and go to the airport early. However, she was committed to going to the lunch where Brad was speaking. In a weak moment, she'd promised him she'd critique his speech. Of course, she'd made the promise in between rounds of sex when it would have been impossible to deny him any request.

The problem with trying to get some sleep was, instead of thinking about her day tomorrow, all she could think about was the evening she'd spent with Brad. The man was a superb lover. She'd actually made notes when she first got back to her room so she could use some of his moves in her next book. The sex scenes between her heroine and hero would be easy to write thanks to Brad Davis and the way he took possession of her body and made it sing. That wasn't an exaggeration. If anyone had been listening, they would certainly have heard the music. Of course if she didn't get some sleep, the bags under her eyes and the pasty color of her skin would let everyone in on the secret. No listening would be required.

Maybe if she replayed some of the highlights of their evening, she might drift off into a racy, steamy dream. Maybe her dreams would bring some color to her cheeks.

• • •

Claire looked startled to see Brad when he knocked on her door at seven thirty the next morning. "Good morning. I didn't expect to see you at …" She looked over her shoulder but couldn't seem to see the clock. "… At this hour. Did we make plans for this morning?"

Brad ducked his head and lightly kissed her cheek. "Nope. No plans. Just had the need to see you again. Are you going down for breakfast?" It registered that she was dressed but hadn't put on any makeup or her fake glasses. She looked sweeter, less sophisticated than she did in full April Mayes mode, but still lovely. This morning, she seemed to have color in her cheeks even without blusher. He hoped he knew why.

"I was but I'm not quite ready."

"I'll wait for you, if you don't mind." He settled in the chair nearest the TV, which she had turned on to CNN. "What's going on in the world this morning?"

"The usual bad weather, civil wars, and political pontifications. Nothing out of the ordinary." As she walked past him, headed for the bathroom, he grabbed her hand and pulled her into his lap. "Hey, I'll never be ready for breakfast if you do things like that."

He cupped her face in his hands. "I'm suddenly less interested in breakfast than I am in kissing you. Do you mind?" He didn't wait for an answer but claimed her mouth in a kiss that started out sweet but moved quickly to hot and possessive.

She pulled back long before he was ready to give up the kiss. "I don't think this is a good idea. I mean, kissing you is a great idea. But not now. I have a workshop right after breakfast, and you have your after-lunch speech to prep for. If we keep going ..."

"We'll blow off the whole convention and give everyone attending a great piece of gossip to take home to their RWA chapter meetings."

His comment seemed to startle her. She jumped up from his lap and, without looking back, headed for the bathroom, closing the door firmly when she got there.

He laughed and lounged back in the chair. The news, as April ... or Claire ... said, wasn't very interesting. It held his attention for all of two minutes before he began to scan the room. Her suitcase was on the luggage stand, the top up so he could see the neat row of shoes in the bottom of the bag. A white plastic bag was visible in the mesh compartment in the top. There was no evidence of other clothes. She was obviously someone who unpacked everything, unlike his approach, which was to live out of the suitcase, his clothing getting messier and more wrinkled as the week went on.

A messenger bag, two books, and the materials from the conference goodie bag were in neat piles on the table next to him. Another book was next to her bed. All three were literary bestsellers.

Most interesting, however, was the tangled mess of sheets on the bed. Had she had as restless a night as he had? He hoped so. He'd had one hell of a night wondering when he'd have the chance to repeat their evening together. It had been the most amazing night of his life. He didn't care if she was a natural at sex, if she'd researched it for her books, or if she'd had enough experience to make her so good at it. Frankly, all he cared about was figuring a way to make it happen again. Preferably as soon as he could. Like tonight.

When she reappeared, she was made up and had her glasses on. "I'm ready, if you are," she said as she picked up her messenger bag and slung it over her shoulder.

If only she knew what he was ready for, she might not be so willing to give him such a big, warm smile.

•••

"I see you made up for not knowing who he was." For the second time in less than two hours, Claudia was startled by the appearance of someone she didn't expect. She had just finished breakfast with Brad and was headed for the room where the panel she was on would be when her agent snuck up behind her.

"For heavens sake, Mary Lynn, I thought you were sleeping in this morning. Don't be so furtive. You'll get my adrenaline going, and I won't be able to think straight when I'm supposed to be lucid and helpful."

"I cannot imagine any circumstance under which you would be unable to be both of those things. And you didn't respond to my comment."

"Because I have no idea what you're talking about."

"I saw you at breakfast with a certain hot historical romance writer and wondered ..."

"Our tables were next to one another at the book signing, and we got talking. He's interesting. We ... ah ... ran into each other this morning. That's all."

"If I'd known the book signing got me next to him, I'd have stayed and given you a run for your money."

Claudia cocked her head and pursed her mouth, tapping her lips with her forefinger. "Hmm. A fellow agent on the plane. My editor last night at dinner. Now Brad Davis. You collecting men?"

"Of course not. I'm happily unattached and intend to remain so."

Claudia could swear Mary Lynn was a rosier color than normal. "Who's making you blush—the agent, the editor, or the author?"

"None of your damn business. Let it go. You have to be in the front of the room in less than ten minutes." Mary Lynn took Claudia's elbow and practically pushed her into the meeting room. Claudia tucked away for future use the information that she could get her agent off track by mentioning a couple of men.

The panel discussion went well. Claudia noticed Brad slip in and sit at the back of the room as the introductions were being made. He grinned at her when he caught her eye. She couldn't help it; she grinned back, hoping Mary Lynn wasn't paying attention.

Just before the session was over, Brad made a quiet exit from the room. She wondered if he was honoring her request to keep her personal life out of the range of anyone who might gossip. It was thoughtful of him, if he was, indeed, protecting her. Of course, after last night, if he kept her personal life quiet this morning, it meant he was keeping his under wraps, too.

Unfortunately, Mary Lynn was all too aware of what had happened. Two minutes after the panel was over, she grabbed her client. "He came to hear you speak? Seems like more than a casual interest to me. And before you tell me he was here to find out where the market's headed, stop yourself. He doesn't write for a market, he created his own."

"We were talking about the subject at breakfast, and he wanted to hear what the others had to stay."

"Right. The others. That's why your face lit up like a spotlight when he smiled at you."

"Did not."

"Did, too. I thought you said you weren't interested in him."

"I enjoyed talking to him." She crossed her fingers as she told the lie, hoping she didn't sound too defensive. No way in hell was she going to confess to the night she'd spent in his bed.

"Okay, honey. You keep thinking it's only his conversation." Mary Lynn patted her on the arm. "I'm not much interested in anything else today. Want to leave early and get lunch someplace outside the hotel before we head for the airport?"

A half dozen more lies flew around Claudia's head but none of them seemed logical, even to her. So she was stuck with the truth. "Actually, I'd like to stay for lunch here and then leave."

"Why would you eat another convention meal when you could ...?" Mary Lynn pulled the conference program from the huge shoulder bag she always carried. Claudia never could figure out how she seemed able to get exactly what she wanted without having to rummage. "Wait. I bet ..." She flipped through the pages. "Yup. Thought so. You want to hear him speak, don't you?"

"Yes, damn it. I do. So sue me."

Mary Lynn laughed, then seemed to be about to say something else when a male voice interrupted.

"Claire? You going to the next session? Want some company?" Brad called from across the room.

For the first time in her life, Claudia understood what people meant when they said their stomachs dropped. She wasn't sure she'd get hers back to its normal place in her belly anytime before lunch, it felt so out of place.

Mary Lynn's eyebrows almost hit her hairline. "Claire? What the hell ...?"

Claudia gripped her agent's arm so tightly she was sure she was leaving fingerprints. "Play along with me, please. I'm begging. I'll explain later. But not here. When we get away from the conference."

Before she could say any more, Brad was in front of her. "Your session was good. I learned a lot. Might think about writing historical-zombie-romance. Sounds like there's a market."

"The problem is, by the time you write to the markets they were talking about, readers will be on to something else," Mary Lynn said. She put out her hand. "Hi, I'm Mary Lynn Elliot. I'm Cl ..."

"Claire's agent. I recognize you. I'm Brad Davis."

"Of course you are. I'm a fan. I particularly loved your latest. Abigail Scott Duniway was a piece of work, wasn't she?"

He smiled, and Claudia could swear Mary Lynn began to visibly melt. A twinge of an unfamiliar emotion tweaked the back of her mind. She couldn't be jealous. Could she?

Mary Lynn did her usual and held on to the handshake with both hands. "I'm looking forward to hearing you at lunch." She dropped his hand and turned to her client. "If you'll excuse me, I'll leave you two kids for a while. Save me a place at lunch, will you? I'm going back to my room to pack and answer some texts."

Claudia let out a long breath. Another bullet dodged. "To answer your original question," she began, "I was headed for the panel on romantic suspense. The next release I'm working on verges on suspense, and I thought I'd hear what the experts have to say about it."

"Not my field, but if you'll sit at the back of the room with me and let me whisper inappropriate things in your ear while I stroke your soft skin, I'll join you."

Chapter 9

Seated in the main ballroom waiting for lunch and her agent, Claudia tried to remember what she'd heard in the last session. Nothing came to mind. Well, nothing except the outrageous things Brad Davis had whispered to her about what they had done the night before and what he wanted to do with her the next time they were alone. Her hormones were in overdrive from his words. She had come close to suggesting they ditch lunch and head for her room. Until she remembered he was the after-lunch speaker and it would be only too obvious if he didn't show up.

"Penny for your thoughts, lovely." The sound of his voice whispering close to her ear again sent more shivers through her already sensitized body.

"Just trying to sort through what I heard in the last session."

She didn't have to see it to guess his sinful smile had appeared. He sat down and whispered even closer to her ear, "And I'll bet this year's royalties none of it had anything to do with romantic suspense. Unless the suspense was when we would be able implement some of the suggestions I made."

"You're awfully sure of yourself, aren't you? Maybe I was thinking about my next book."

"Which part of your next book? The part where the hero and heroine are ..."

"I've been looking all over for you, Mr. Davis. And here you are, right on time and in the right place. I might have known you would be here. You're so reliable." Lucinda Pennington, the meeting organizer, interrupted.

Claudia almost laughed. He must get that all the time.

"I hate to break up your conversation with Ms. Mayes," Lucinda continued. "But I'd like to show you to the head table so you can meet our president, who'll be introducing you."

It was gratifying to Claudia to see how slowly Brad rose from his chair. "Duty calls, Cl ... April. Will I see you after lunch?"

"Mary Lynn and I will probably sneak out during the Q and A so we can get checked out. We're leaving on the four o'clock flight."

"If I'd known when you were flying, I would have changed my flight so we could all go to the airport together. But as it is, I'm meeting some old friends this afternoon and flying out later tonight."

Thank you, God. He wouldn't be at the airport to see her real name or find out she was flying into Portland, too. Another bullet dodged. There were so many potential deadly missiles out there with her name on them, it was beginning to feel like she was in a war zone.

"Next time we're both on the program at a conference, we should coordinate our flights so we arrive at the same time," he continued. "Give us a chance to have a drink or something before we get to the convention hotel." He leaned over, and Claudia held her breath, afraid he would actually kiss her in front of the convention organizer. Instead he took her hand and squeezed it. "Make good use of my e-mail address, won't you?"

"I promise." She wasn't sure if she would, or if it was one more lie to add to the others she'd told the man over the past twenty-four hours.

• • •

He was a brilliant speaker, without question. In only a few sentences, he had the entire audience, including everyone at her table, in the palm of his hand. He was funny, informative, and very, very sexy with his deep voice, slightly suggestive comments, and complete command of his subject matter. If she could have, she'd have signed up for his classes at St. Mary's to hear him talk some more.

Claudia was sorry when the Q and A session began, and Mary Lynn nudged her and nodded toward the door. "I'm sure you want to stay and listen to him flirt with all the women in the audience," she said in a quiet tone. "But let's get out of here so you can fill me in on what the hell is going on with you and him."

"Keep your voice down! Nothing's going on. You're imagining things."

Mary Lynn whispered back. "Nothing? Let's see—you drooled over him in the bar. Came back and had a drink with him last night. There's enough heat generated when the two of you look at each other to warm what's left of the polar ice cap. And for some reason, he thinks your name is Claire. That's a lot of nothing. And I want the details of all of it."

"How do you know about last night?"

"That's all you have to say? Hmm. Interesting. I'll pursue the rest later. The answer to your question is: I have my sources. They were in the bar last night, too. I'm always looking out for the interests of my clients. And what went on last night may or may not be in the best interest of one of my favorite clients."

"Okay, okay. I get it. You're protecting my interests."

"Which I can do more easily if I know exactly what happened between the two of you."

"Right. It's not curiosity and the love of gossip." She waved off what was likely to be Mary Lynn's next rationalization for knowing what happened with Brad by saying, "Fine. I'll tell you when we get to the airport. Let's get out of here without drawing any more attention to ourselves than you already have."

• • •

Brad watched as Claire and her agent walked out the back door, closing it quietly so it didn't disrupt the question an earnest fan was asking him. He almost lost the thread of what she was saying so intent was he on soaking up the last glimpse of the woman who had fascinated him from the first time he'd seen her.

The thing was, even after their night together and the conversations they'd had over the past couple days, he didn't feel like he'd gotten any more clues about who she really was, which made him more intrigued, not less. And even more determined to solve the puzzle. He wasn't happy any further contact hinged on her making the first move. But she set the rules. He would live with it. Until he didn't hear from her. Then he'd track her down if he had to call every phone number he could get his hands on for Bellevue College until he found someone who could tell him how to get in touch with her.

•••

"Right. We're away from the conference. Spill. What went on between you and Brad Davis, and why did he call you Claire?"

Claudia and Mary Lynn had settled into the frequent flyer lounge and ordered a glass of wine. Since their flight was still several hours away and Claudia hadn't a snowball's chance in hell of evading her agent's questions, she took a deep breath and started, hoping to bury her friend in a flurry of words so she'd shut up.

"We spent most of the night together last night, and I told him my name was Claire Mason because he figured out April Mayes was a pen name, but I didn't want him to know my real name because he's from Portland, too, and thinks I'm from Seattle."

"Wait, wait. Let's start from the beginning. You spent the night with him? In all the years I've known you, you've never done anything like that. At least not to my knowledge. Why him? Why here?"

"It's all your fault. I was trying so hard to act in keeping with the way you'd dressed me up it was easy to be ... well, to be easy."

"Yeah, right. Blame it on me. I had nothing to do with the way you looked at each other this morning. I have to assume what happened was good."

"It was better than anything I've ever written."

"Jesus. I *should* have made a move if he's that good. I've read your stuff."

"I'd really rather you didn't."

"That's all you have to say? You'd really rather I didn't? I'd expect more like you'd scratch my eyes out.'"

"I don't want to look for another agent." Claudia took a sip of her wine. A big sip, hoping the whole "vino veritas" thing would work in her favor. "Truth is, I don't really have any claim on him. It could be we had a convention fling. Like the one in my *A Series of Errors*."

"He didn't look at you like it was a conference hookup. Did he ask for your contact info?"

"Of course. I avoided answering him. I got his, though." She patted her messenger bag. "I haven't decided what to do with it.'

"Oh, yes, you have. Don't try to kid yourself. It's written all over your face every time you look at him." Mary Lynn leaned across the table. "But what's with the Claire-from-Seattle business? Why didn't you give him your real name? Why did you have to invent yet another name?"

"He saw me at Sea-Tac and assumed, since I was flying from there, that I live in Seattle. And I kinda slipped up and almost said my real name. The first two letters were all I got out but he picked up on it and nagged me about until I told him it was Claire."

"Still don't understand why you didn't tell him the truth."

"He teaches at St. Mary's. In Portland. Two blocks away from Portland State. He guest lectures at my university. In my boss's class. He probably uses our library for his research. And if not there, then at the Historical Society, which is right next door to

PSU. For all I know, he walks every day in the Park Blocks and knows half the faculty."

"So?"

"So? So, he could blab, tell people how we met, what I write. I can't chance it."

"But he writes romance, too."

"He's a man. He writes respectable books. I'm not and I don't."

"Who cares? You're a success. You write beautifully. Your books are based on Shakespeare or Austen stories. How can anyone object?"

"You don't know the vagaries of a tenure committee. They're unpredictable. All it takes is one or two people who don't think you live up to the standards of the department, and you're doomed. And the tenure committee has Statler and Waldorf."

"Who the hell are they?"

"A couple old-school professors who don't like commercial fiction, don't think academics should write it, and would organize a mob of like-minded snobs to come drag me off to the ducking stool if they knew I did. I have worked my whole professional life for this shot at tenure. It's important. Maybe the most important thing I'll ever achieve. I won't let my extra-curricular writing get in the way."

"Don't you think Brad would understand if you explained it to him?"

"I can't take a chance."

"So you invented another name. Which makes three: one for your friends, family, and colleagues; one for your readers; and one for Brad Davis. Am I the only one who knows them all?"

Hearing what she'd done described by someone else made it sound so much worse than it had seemed a few minutes ago. "Yes, I guess you're right. Although when you say it, it sounds much worse than it did in my head."

"Interesting." Mary Lynn's eyebrows almost blended into her bangs. "Instead of coming clean about your beautiful writing, you've added another layer of hiding. Why would you do that rather than just admit who you are when you write novels?"

"Don't get any bright ideas about pressuring me to go public about April. You can't make me. And you don't dare sink me because if you did, you'd sink a healthy part of your income."

"For God's sake, Claudia. Do you think I'd do something so low? You know I'd never hurt you. You certainly began as my client, but you're my friend now, and I protect my friends." Mary Lynn drained the last of her wine and set the glass back down on the table. "Now that you've created this fantasy female for Mr. Davis, what do you plan to do with her?"

Claudia groaned. "I don't know. I want to see him again, but I don't know how to do it without giving it all away."

Mary Lynn was silent for a long time. At least it seemed like a long time to Claudia. "I almost hate myself for what I'm about to say," she finally began. "But I saw the way you looked at each other and, honey, there's something there you shouldn't let go of. I'm not sure I should suggest this, but maybe there's a way you could see him again without telling him you're really Claudia Manchester."

"How? I've tried to think of some way to run into him accidently but can't come up with something other than some lame coincidence. I suppose I could wait until we go to Denver to RWA, but the conference is too far off. I want to see him before then."

"I agree. My idea flies in the face of everything I said about the situation, but it's the only way I can see for you to get together with him soon. It would be a test of your acting skills. But you did okay pretending in San Fran."

"Come on, Mary Lynn. Spit it out."

"How about this? How about you go whole hog into this Claire-from-Seattle thing? Create the rest of your new persona— get a new e-mail, a Seattle area phone number ..."

"But he wants to come see me. How can I do that when I don't have a place in Seattle? And don't tell me to rent an apartment there. I can barely afford Portland, let alone a second place."

"Let me finish. You can use my address. You've stayed at my house often enough. You should feel somewhat at home there. I'm out of town on business pretty often. You'd have a place to stay in Seattle where you can entertain him and my car with Washington plates you can drive him around in."

"I don't know my way around the city very well."

"That's what Google and GPS are for. Besides, from the way he looks at you, I very much doubt he has sightseeing in mind when he's with you."

Now it was Claudia's turn to be quiet while she thought about the idea. Finally, she said, "Do you really think it'll work?"

"Has my advice ever failed you?"

"About my literary life, no. But I've never asked you for advice about my personal life."

"I'm just as good there. Trust me." Mary Lynn dipped into her bag and brought out a notebook and a pen. "Let's start making lists of what you need to do to pull this off."

•••

It didn't take long to establish Claudia's new identity as Claire Mason. In fact, it was frighteningly easy. Claudia kept telling herself it was all research for a future book. Shakespeare must have done similar research when he wrote all his mistaken identity comedies, she decided. Well, except for the phone and e-mail trails. He wouldn't have had to worry about those things. But rationalizing she was following in the footsteps of the Bard faded away when she remembered she was doing it so she could have another weekend with Brad. Then any reluctance disappeared in a haze of desire.

After less than a week, everything was in place and Claudia wrote an e-mail to Brad using her new Gmail account. Her first draft read:

How was your flight home? Mary Lynn and I made it back without incident. Sorry it took so long to get in touch. It's been hectic since I got home. If you still want to get together, how about coming up to Seattle in a couple weeks? Assuming your schedule works. And, like I said, you still want to.

Oh, hell. Erase. Erase. Erase. That wasn't how she wanted to come across. It sounded like a mash-up between something she'd write to one of her friends and a middle school girl writing to her crush. Try again.

See? I'm making good use of your e-mail address. Here's my cell number: 425-000-9876. And, of course, you now know my e-mail address. Let me know you got this.

Claire

There. Better. She read it through twice, moved a comma or two, and hit "send." The ball was in his court. If he wanted to see her, he would answer. If he didn't, he could …

Before she could finish the thought, the burner phone Mary Lynn had sent her, so he wouldn't see a Portland area code, buzzed. She had a text.

Got it, lovely. Can I see you this weekend? I'll come to Seattle. Or meet you wherever.

Her heart was beating so hard she could feel her pulse in her thumbs, which made answering the text something of a challenge. Finally, after massive editing and overriding autocorrect a dozen times, she got off a response.

This weekend would be great. I'll send you an e-mail with directions to the house. Will you get here Saturday morning?

The response came back even faster than the first one had.

Can't wait 'til Saturday. Friday night about 8 or so. Late dinner?

Claudia stared at the response for a long time. She was happy Brad was so eager to see her again; she was excited to see him. But there was another emotion roiling around. One she didn't recognize at first.

Finally she texted back:

I'll have dinner waiting for you.

When she turned her phone off, the other feeling rose to the surface and burst, not like a bubble but like a bomb. The enormity of what she was about to do hit her, and she was scared spitless about whether she could pull it off.

Not for the first time with this man, she wondered what she was doing.

•••

During the summer, Claudia's teaching schedule was light to nonexistent. This summer in particular, she wasn't committed to much more than a few guest lectures and some mentoring sessions with a couple of her graduate students. And since she usually tried to have Friday afternoons free, she had a convenient way to escape for a weekend away. This weekend, in particular, she was happy she'd planned her summer that way.

As soon as her writing hours in the morning were over, she headed for her car. Her suitcase had been packed the night before, full of some of the clothes she'd worn in San Francisco along with a newly acquired sexy nightgown, sneakers, a pair of jeans, and a couple of turtleneck sweaters. She believed in being ready for anything.

All she had to do was get through the traffic to Mary Lynn's home, get her things in the right place in the bedroom, get dinner started, and she'd be ready for Brad's arrival. At least, as ready as she was likely to ever be, given that she was about to try to pull off the biggest con of her life.

When Mary Lynn first suggested the idea of creating a Claire Mason identity, it had sounded fun. A challenge. Then, as she put in place the pieces of her "new" self and it had gotten more real, she made notes about what she was doing in case she really did want to use it as a storyline for a future book. Now, however, she was beginning to wonder exactly what it said about her that she was so willing to continue to fool—all right, *lie*—to this man she found so compellingly attractive.

The easy answer was, she had to protect her reputation until after she had tenure. She couldn't take a chance on Brad letting something about her slip to someone at St. Mary's who knew someone at Portland State. Or, even worse, to her boss when he was guest teaching. Then there were the teachers she knew at most of the schools in Portland who might also know him. Portland was a very small town in many ways, and they were bound to have acquaintances in common. She shuddered to think of all the chances there might be for him to let the information slip about what she wrote, information that would inevitably find its way back to the tenure committee. And, as she'd told Mary Lynn, she'd worked hard for tenure for more years than she cared to count, and she didn't want to blow it now when it was so close.

But deep inside, she knew there was another reason. One she hesitated to admit. She was afraid if Brad Davis, Mr. Hot and Handsome, knew she was boring Claudia Manchester, PhD, he wouldn't be nearly as interested in her as he was in April Mayes/Claire Mason. Oh, he said he was attracted to her brains as well as her body, but men say things like that if they think it'll score points with a woman. At least, in her experience. Even the man with whom she'd had the torrid affair, the one that had inspired her first book, a man who had wined and dined her, taken her on trips to Seattle and Las Vegas, and had brought her enough flowers to stock a small florist ... even he had admitted, eventually, how intimidated he was by her intelligence and her advanced degree. He only had a master's.

It wasn't the reason they called it off. But it was the reason they had never gotten beyond the friends-with-benefits stage, she was sure.

Then there was the fascination Brad seemed to have for what she wrote. She had always been afraid people—specifically, men—would look at her differently if they knew what kind of romances she wrote. Granted, Brad admitted he'd never read any of her books, but, hey, all he had to do was look at the covers to know exactly what was inside. And he'd had plenty of time to look at the covers of her books while they were sitting side by side at the book signing. Was his attraction to her based on some fantasy about who he thought a steamy romance writer was?

Of course there was her own fantasy about living life dangerously, like one of her heroines. She had felt so alive when they'd connected at the conference, so much like something out of a book, not out of her rather routine life. Was she using Brad to fulfill her own ideas of what an exciting romance was?

All of this consumed her thoughts as she drove north for the second weekend in a row. The Saturday before, she'd stayed overnight with Mary Lynn, at her agent's suggestion, to accustom herself to the house. She'd stayed there before but had never, for example, slept in the master bedroom. Mary Lynn spent two days drilling her on where everything like fresh towels, the corkscrew, silverware, and pots were. Sunday afternoon, when Mary Lynn cross-examined her on what she knew about the house, it felt like the orals for her doctorate all over again except, this time, she'd had only a few hours to prepare.

On her way out of Portland, Claudia stopped by the grocery store to pick up a few things to add to what she'd seen in Mary Lynn's pantry. For dinner, she planned to cook her favorite chicken cacciatore with a salad and a nice wine. And she wanted to have plenty on hand for breakfast on Saturday and Sunday.

Breakfast. Brad would be there for breakfast. He'd be spending the night. Two nights. The thought made her shiver in anticipation. If what she was presenting as her life was a charade, it was some comfort that at least she was being honest with him when they were in bed.

Traffic wasn't too bad heading into Seattle. She got to Mary Lynn's house with plenty of time to do what she needed to do to carry out her plan. First, she parked two blocks away from the house so a car with Oregon plates wouldn't be in the driveway. Next, she put her clothes in the closet and in bureau drawers. Luckily, she and Mary Lynn were much the same size so clothes that didn't belong to her looked as if they could. Her feet were smaller than her agent's were so she hid the collection of boots and shoes from the master bedroom in the guest room.

After that was all settled, she put her own iPod into the dock in the living room, so she didn't have to explain anyone else's taste in music. And added her favorite wine and Scotch to supplement what was already there.

When she was sure every place in the house looked like it might be her home, she changed into jeans and one of the turtlenecks. April Mayes's artificial nails were long gone, as were her hennaed extensions. Mary Lynn had volunteered to get her made over again, but Claudia had turned down the offer. To retain some shred of integrity, she wanted Brad to know at least some part of who she really was, even if it was only the cosmetic changes she'd made for San Francisco. It was taking a chance. But if Brad was only attracted to her in the Queen of Steam costume, she wanted to know.

With her clothes and the scene all settled, she started the sauce for the chicken, tossed the salad, and poured a glass of wine for herself. Then she put on the music she usually used when she was meditating and waited.

She didn't have to wait long. Brad must have flown up the freeway because when the doorbell rang, it was not yet seven thirty. Opening the door, she found Mr. Hot and Handsome standing there, a backpack over one leather-clad shoulder and a big grin on his face.

"Hi." She hated how her throat closed at the sight of him, making her greeting come out in a squeak.

"Hi? That's all I get after fighting through the Friday traffic in Portland, Tacoma, and Seattle? Don't I deserve something better?" He stepped inside the door and pushed it closed with his rear end.

After swallowing a couple of times and licking her lips, Claudia said, "Okay. Hi, I'm glad to see you. Better?"

"Not really. This is more what I had in mind." In a smooth motion, he dropped the pack on the floor with one hand and drew her against him with the other. Before she could register that she was in his arms again and loved being there, his mouth came down on her and she tasted the sweet maleness of him, mixed with the scent of fresh air and a spicy smell from some aftershave or shower gel. She moaned, and he slid his hands down her back to her rear, snugging her against him so there was nothing between their bodies but thin layers of clothes. She could feel the heat from his body, the firm muscles of his chest. The hard thickness of an erection began to press against her stomach.

Her arms twined around his neck as he thoroughly explored every bit of her mouth, his tongue making promises of what she knew would come later in the evening. By the time he lifted his head and touched his forehead to hers, she was breathing raggedly and so was he.

"Now you can say hi," he whispered.

She coughed. "I'm not sure I can speak coherently."

"Good. That's what I was going for."

...

Brad had left Portland as soon as he could, after a class he was teaching every afternoon at the Oregon Historical Society on how to do historical research. It wasn't early enough to suit him, but unfortunately, it was the way it worked out. Traffic on I-5 north to Washington State was the usual slow crawl, but almost magically, once he cleared Clark County, things moved along at the speed limit. Even the dreaded Tacoma Dome curves weren't too bad, and he must have missed the end of shift at Joint Base Lewis-McChord because it wasn't too bad there, either. Only when he was creeping past Boeing Field, with Seattle in sight, did things get dicey. Even so, he made it to Claire's door more than a half hour earlier than he expected.

She was as lovely as he remembered, as sexy as his dreams had made her out to be. In fact, in bare feet, jeans, and a turtleneck sweater, her face scrubbed of makeup and the fake glasses nowhere in sight, she looked even better than she had in San Francisco.

"You've cut your hair," he said, bringing some of it from behind her ear where he'd noticed she'd nervously tucked it after she answered the door. "And it's not as red as I remember it."

She looked startled at his comment, almost afraid. "Yes, it's sort of different. I guess. Is it so noticeable?"

"It looks great. I thought you'd be impressed I noticed." He couldn't let her go quite yet, although she looked like she needed to move away from him. It was cute she was nervous.

He took her hand, picked up his backpack, and asked, "Where shall I put this?"

"I'll take it. And put it in the ... in my room." Avoiding his eyes, she made good on her word and disappeared down a hall.

As he shed his leather jacket, he took the chance to look around at her home. It was a small, cozy Craftsman house, his favorite northwest architectural style. The built-in bookcases in the living room were filled with books, which he would have expected. The art on the walls was a surprise, though. It consisted of fussy still life pictures of fruit and flowers, not the kind of work he thought Claire might like. In fact, the more he looked around at the living and dining rooms, the more puzzled he was. The furniture was upholstered in a cream colored fabric covered in huge, overblown roses. The dining room table had a runner down the center in a similar pattern. The hardwood floors were the only relief from the flowers and fruit that were everywhere else.

Not at all what he expected. But then, hadn't Claire been completely unexpected in almost every way since he met her?

"I was having a glass of wine while I waited for you. Would you like one?"

He hadn't heard her return to the living room, but there she was, in arm's reach again. So his arms reached. "More of this first, I think. Then wine." He kissed her, wanting to do more than give her a sweet kiss but also wanting her to make the move first to deepen their connection.

She did. It was her mouth that demanded more. Her arms that tightened around him. Her hands that pulled his hips into hers. It was what he had fantasized all the way up I-5. And more.

It was also Clair who broke the kiss this time. "I have a little bit left to do for dinner. Come into the kitchen with me and keep me company."

• • •

Claudia brought the chicken, which she had already sautéed, out of the refrigerator and began to arrange it in the pan of sauce bubbling gently on the stove. "Why don't you pour yourself some wine?" she asked, wanting more than anything to find a topic of conversation other than one with the potential to end up with her kissing him again. Or included his noticing how different she was from her April Mayes persona. That almost scared her more than his finding out about her PhD. She was still worried that he was attracted only to the woman who had hair extensions and wore fake cat-eye glasses, although the two kisses had gone some way to allaying her fears.

He picked up a bottle of wine from the counter. "Do you mind if I open this one even if we're having chicken? It's one of my favorite reds."

She looked over her shoulder, saw he had found one her favorites, and nodded. "Be my guest."

He opened a few drawers, rummaging around in each one. "I give up. Where do you keep your corkscrew?"

She panicked for a moment, drawing a blank. Where did Mary Lynn keep the damn thing? She couldn't remember even though it was one of the items she'd been tested on a week before.

"Oh, never mind. It was out on the counter." He opened the bottle and filled the glass she had put out for him. After he took a healthy slug of wine, he leaned one hip against the kitchen counter and smiled. "It smells amazing in here. What are you cooking?"

"It's the tomato sauce for my favorite chicken dish." She looked around for a moment, found the large spoon she needed, and grabbed it. When she tasted the sauce and licked her lips, she saw his eyes widen. "Would you like a taste?" She scooped up more of the sauce and extended the spoon to him.

"Of the sauce or of you?"

"Tasting the sauce was what I meant," she said.

"Tasting you again has been on my mind for days. You've been damn distracting." He took the two steps he needed to get next to her, covered her hand with his, and guided the spoon toward his mouth. "But this'll do. For the moment." His gaze holding hers the whole time, he very efficiently licked the spoon clean.

She needed to swallow hard and moisten her lips again as she watched, a memory of how it felt to have him lick her quickening her heartbeat.

"It's delicious. No wonder it's your favorite."

Leaving her holding the spoon in the air, wearing what she was sure was a stunned expression, he returned to his perch across the room.

"So," he said, "this is your home. It's lovely. But I would have never guessed you were a fan of cabbage roses and still life art."

She was relieved at the change of subject even if it was to Mary Lynn's terrible taste in decorating. Not that she could say much on the subject without giving the game away. But at least she could focus on something other than his mouth, her lips, and the two meeting in another of his blazing kisses.

It was safer to answer his question with her back to him so she returned to the task of covering the chicken breasts with sauce in the pan. "Oh ... um ... really? What would you have guessed my home would look like?"

"Let's see. I thought your furniture might be more sensual, tactile. Velvet? Maybe burgundy colored. Something like that. And the art would show lots of feeling. Not be so formal. Photography, perhaps."

She was stunned at how close he was. The antique love seat in her living room was covered in dark purple velvet, and her walls were hung with black and white photographs of scenes with emotional appeal for her. Some were dramatic shots of scenery. One was of lovers silhouetted in the moonlight. Several were shots of children. "Sorry to disappoint you."

"Not disappointed. Surprised. But then you are constantly surprising me. How long have you owned the place?"

She could have kicked herself for focusing so much on where things were in the house and not preparing herself for the most obvious of questions. "Not long. That is, I don't own the house." She was so nervous, the chicken breast she was burying in the sauce slid across the pan and splashed tomato sauce on her.

Before she could reach for it, he had a paper towel ready for her. As she blotted the sauce off her sweater, she tried again to answer his question. "What I mean is, Mary Lynn owns the house." *At least in the grand scheme of the con she was trying to pull off, something she was telling him was true.*

"You rent from your agent? You must be awfully good friends to have such a close relationship."

"We've become good friends as well as agent and author."

"She's Seattle-based, isn't she?"

"Yes, although she's gone a lot at conferences and back to New York pretty regularly."

"Is she in town this weekend? Maybe we could have brunch or something tomorrow. My agent is about to retire. I'll be looking for a new one shortly but I haven't clicked with any of the other agents he's suggested."

Brunch with Mary Lynn would be the very last thing on the list of things she'd suggest they do this weekend. "She's actually in Portland right now. Not sure if it's business or social." *And not sure if she's having as nervous a time in my house as I'm having in hers.*

"But I'll certainly tell her to get in touch with you. She'd love to talk about representing you, I'm sure."

"If you knew she was headed for Portland, you could have carpooled down with her and stayed at my place."

"Both of us?"

He laughed. "No, I meant *you*. Just you." He finished off the glass of wine and poured himself another one. "But maybe next weekend, you'll come see me. What do you think?"

There was no way in hell she was going to agree to see him in Portland. Not next weekend. Not the weekend after. Not ever. But kissing him had reminded her she was living her heroine's life. Regretting what she *did*. Not what she *didn't* do. Although she had to admit she was storing up future regrets for what she did in an impressive way lately.

Maybe there was a way to get around his request. With her back to him, she couldn't see the expression on his face, wasn't sure she wanted to see how he reacted to what she was about to say. "Actually, I was thinking of going to the coast next weekend. A friend has a place on the Long Beach peninsula I borrow sometimes. It's a good place to write, I've learned." *And it has the advantage of being far enough away from Portland to be safe.*

"Could I join you? I promise I won't interfere with your writing too much. I'm working on a new book myself."

It had taken him exactly five seconds to respond to her invitation to come to Seattle. And even less to ask if he could join her at the coast. She knew she was probably going to hurt his feelings if she took too long to answer, but she had to consider the possible consequences of seeing him two weekends in a row.

Then she remembered the kiss in the entryway. Dear God, he was good at kissing. What harm could come from one more weekend of playing the game out? If she was successful, he'd never twig to the truth. Or maybe they'd get to be on such good terms she could find a way to tell him the truth about who she was. Make a big joke about it. Let him in on the secret so he felt special. Yeah, that's what she'd work for. Making him feel special.

"Sure. I'd love company. I can give you directions before you leave." She finished settling the chicken in the sauce and covered the pan. "It'll be about twenty minutes before we eat." Turning back to him, she asked, "What do you ...?"

The rest of the sentence was lost as his mouth claimed hers once again.

• • •

Damn, the woman drove him crazy. She had actually thought about whether they should spend next weekend together before she answered. He needed to kiss her until she knew, as he did, that every minute spent away from each other was a wasted minute and every chance they had to be together should be grabbed with both hands and held tight. It had only taken a couple days with her in San Francisco to realize how much he wanted to have more time with her.

He deepened the kiss, slicking his tongue over hers, exploring her mouth, nibbling at her lips. She moaned against his mouth, and he felt her mold her body to his. His erection was now rock hard and ready to explore her body the way his hands were. They were busy moving under her sweater, reminding him how soft and smooth her skin was.

"Can I take this thing off?" he asked, tugging up on her sweater.

"If I can do the same with you."

She had his shirt unbuttoned before he could get the sweater over her head. When he did, he was delighted to discover she wore no bra. She returned to kissing him when they were both bare-chested. Her nipples were tight and hard against him.

He reached between them for the snap on her jeans, trying to maintain the kiss while he struggled to get the zipper down. She giggled.

"Stop laughing and help me, woman," he said.

She shimmied out of her jeans and panties and tried to kiss him again, but he wouldn't let her. "I want to look at you." He picked her up and set her on the nearest counter. She gasped, as if surprised, and licked her lips in anticipation of his kiss. But instead of her mouth, he claimed the pulse at the base of her throat, then moved up to her jawline, then to her ear where he whispered, "Sweet Jesus, mother of God, you are beautiful."

He pulled her hips forward and spread her legs. Taking her mouth in another kiss, he slowly caressed her thighs, moving ever closer to her sex as he did. When she moaned against his mouth again, he turned his attention to her breasts, going from one nipple to another, massaging, turning them to tight peaks.

She was arching her back and her fingers were tangled in his hair as he dropped to his knees and carefully parted the folds of her sex before dipping one finger, then another, into her hot, wet core.

She gasped again, her head fell back, and she opened her legs further.

With his tongue he stroked her clitoris as his fingers massaged inside. He felt her internal muscles tighten, heard her breath quicken, saw her eyes close, and then heard her call his name as she climaxed.

He quickly stood and gathered her into his arms. Her head sank onto his shoulder; her arms went around his waist. For several minutes, they stayed entwined until her breathing was more regular.

She finally sat up straight and sighed. "I've never done that before."

He wasn't quite sure what she meant. "Done what before?"

"Had sex on a kitchen counter." She slid off onto the floor, shook her head as if to clear it, and looked around.

He handed her the jeans and panties from where they'd been dropped at his feet. "Ah, *that*. Well, I'm happy to have given you a new experience."

She returned the favor, picking up his shirt. "But it doesn't seem fair. I had all the fun."

"Oh, no, lovely, not true. I've been thinking about tasting you again for days. I couldn't wait any longer. And it was just as good as I remembered." He buttoned his shirt and tucked it into his jeans.

"Well, I'll make it up to you after dinner."

He snagged her arm as she walked past and gave her one more blazing hot kiss. He thought she was about to make good on her promise right then and there. Until he heard her stomach rumble. Apparently the aroma of the garlic-infused tomato sauce simmering on the stove had given her other ideas.

"Sounds like you need dinner first."

"Yes, well, I haven't eaten since breakfast." She was dressing faster than he'd undressed her, which he thought was a miracle in itself.

"What can I do to help?"

"How about you get the salad out of the refrigerator and put it on the dining room table? There should be a little jug of dressing right next to it. I'll dish up the chicken and join you."

Chapter 10

The dinner was everything she wanted it to be: The food was delicious, the conversation fascinating. They exchanged stories about their week and filled in details about themselves, their backgrounds, and interests. She was able to be completely honest about her work because she'd spent the week writing. And she shared enough about her real background—like where she'd done her undergrad work and how she had taught middle school English while she worked on her master's—to make her comfortable in the knowledge she hadn't lied to him about *everything*. Only a few things. She quickly dismissed the little voice in her head whispering, *"A few things? A few key things, don't you think?"*

He pitched in after dinner and helped clean up the kitchen. By the time they were finished, it was, he said, late and he was ready for bed. The look in his eyes didn't seem to signal he was tired. It did look like he was eager for bed. So was she.

* * *

The rest of the weekend flew by in a haze of good food, a lot of laughing, and almost as much lovemaking. Claudia was on a high for two days, able to keep the horrid voice in her head from reminding her she was lying to this man with every minute about who she was. Even the few times she remembered, she couldn't bring herself to regret it. It was the best two days she'd had since ... well, since San Francisco. And those were the best two days she'd had in years.

The only thing she regretted about the masquerade was he didn't call her name, her *real* name, when they were in bed.

After Brad left on Sunday afternoon, she went through Mary Lynn's house making sure everything was in order and all traces of the pair were gone. She did the laundry, returned all Mary Lynn's shoes and boots to her closet, and put the crap her agent kept on the refrigerator back in place. Then she headed south.

Mary Lynn was still at her house when she got there.

"So, how'd the dirty weekend go?" was how she greeted Claudia.

"Dirty weekend? What the hell do you mean?"

"What I said. Surely an English lit professor recognizes the main plot point from *The Norman Conquests*."

"Of course I know those plays. But I'd forgotten that bit." She dropped her overnight bag on the steps to the second floor. "Besides, it wasn't a dirty weekend. It was ..." She stopped, not sure how to accurately describe what the weekend had meant to her.

"So, there was no sex?"

"Mary Lynn, for God's sake. If you want me to tell you about my weekend, let me tell it in my own way. Yes, there was sex. Fabulous, fantastic, mind-blowing sex. He's-better-than-any-hero-I've-ever-written sex. But it was more than sex. It was ... I don't know ... nice."

"Nice is not a word I'd associate with a dirty weekend."

"I told you. It wasn't like that."

"Then what was it like?"

"I'm not sure I have the words to tell you." She laughed a little. "Which is not the best thing for a writer to admit, is it? But it's true. We clicked on so many levels. Talking with him was as exciting as making love with him. Almost."

"It sounds serious."

"Not yet but maybe ..." An image of Brad's reaction if she told him the truth about who she was made a rude appearance in her head. "Probably not. It's hard to imagine something serious coming from the tangle of lies I've told."

"Do you really think he'd walk away if you told him the truth?"

"After everything I've hidden from him, why wouldn't he?" She began ticking items off on her fingers. "First, I'm sleeping with a man who thinks I'm one of two phony names. Second, I'm doing it at your house because he thinks I live in Seattle. Third, he doesn't know I'm a full professor at Portland State where he sometimes teaches a class for my boss." She threw her hands up in exasperation. "I've faked everything."

"I sincerely hope not, girlfriend." Mary Lynn said.

"I don't mean I'm faking *that*."

"Thank you, Jesus." Mary Lynn put her hand up as if to ward off the next protestation. "But you don't seem to be faking the fact you're falling for the guy. That seems real enough to me."

"I am not falling for him. I'm not foolish enough to do something rash like fall in love. Not with all the conniving it's taken to be together. I'm merely having an adventure. I have no intention of falling for anyone. And I'm sure he's looking for the same thing."

On her way upstairs to the guest room to collect her suitcase and her laptop, Mary Lynn threw the last line back over her shoulder. "You keep telling yourself that, sunshine. Maybe you'll be able to convince yourself of it. In a century or two."

Claudia was so thrown off balance at the thought she might be falling for Brad Davis she forgot to tell Mary Lynn that Brad might be looking for a new agent and wanted to talk to her. When she finally remembered, after Mary Lynn had left, she texted her with his contact information.

It was the least she could do for the woman who was loaning her a place for her dirty weekends.

• • •

The drive back to Portland had never gone by so quickly for Brad as it had on Sunday. Before he could even register that he'd cleared the Puget Sound, he was crossing the I-5 Bridge into Oregon.

The weekend couldn't have gone better. He had feared Claire/ April would retreat from what they'd had in San Francisco, but a flood of great sex and fascinating conversation had washed his concerns away. She was as intriguing, as beautiful, as smart and passionate as she'd been at the conference, and he congratulated himself on his luck at having found such an amazing woman.

There were a couple things he didn't understand. Her house, for one. Not only did the furniture and art not look like anything he could imagine for her, but there were no personal photos anyplace. Nothing displayed on the refrigerator. He hadn't seen a computer either, although he guessed it was possible she wrote her books longhand and had someone transcribe them.

And then there was the mystery of the New Seasons bags. As far as he knew, there were no New Seasons grocery stores in the Seattle area. But there were three brown paper grocery bags with the store's name on them tucked away under the sink. He'd seen them when he'd helped clean up the kitchen. Did she have friends come visit her from Portland laden with groceries? It seemed funny, but he didn't want to ask questions about where her groceries came from.

It was all part of the enigma of this lovely, smart, sexy woman. He'd just have to work harder at unraveling the mystery she presented the following weekend when they'd be writing together at the coast. The next weekend and every chance she gave him until he figured out who this woman was and why he was so fascinated by her.

...

Their time at the beach was as successful as their first weekend in Seattle had been. Maybe even more because Claudia got ten thousand words of her new book written, and Brad had done almost as well even though they kept interrupting their work to make love, to talk, or to walk on the beach. To make it absolutely perfect, it had been a stormy weekend, the kind she loved.

She insisted he leave first saying she would take care of closing up the condo. She didn't want him to see the Oregon license plate on her car, which had been tucked away in the garage under the building all weekend. She'd managed to avoid driving it while he was there and wasn't about to have it all given away when they left. Knowing he was taking Highway 30 on the Oregon side of the Columbia River to get home, she drove on the Washington side of the river, which took longer but would guarantee their paths wouldn't cross until they got to I-5 when it wasn't likely he'd notice her in all the traffic even if they did get there at the same time.

As she replayed the weekend in her head driving the winding road, guilt began to creep into her consciousness. Brad had been so attentive all weekend, so sweet and loving. She should have owned up to who she was, but there hadn't been a good time to set him straight. Actually, she didn't imagine there were many opportunities to do something so potentially embarrassing. How would you even you start *that* conversation? "Oh, speaking of lying to someone you care for, I've been hiding behind a fake identity the whole time we've been making love. Want some more wine?"

And yet if she couldn't find a way to tell him the truth, neither could she bring herself to end it. The sex was great. So was his company. She thought about him more with each passing day. And she was pretty sure, from the way he looked at her, his feelings were getting as involved as hers were. But she'd put herself in an awkward position. The longer it went on, the harder it would be to extricate herself from the web of lies she'd spun, which she'd have to do if she wanted to keep on seeing him, wouldn't she?

They'd made plans to meet in the Columbia River Gorge in two weeks. Maybe that's where she would have the chance to tell him the truth. If he took it well, maybe there could be more.

Assuming they both wanted the same thing. After he learned who she really was.

• • •

To maintain the pretense she was coming from Seattle, on Saturday morning, Claudia drove to the Portland airport, left her car in the parking lot, and took the shuttle to the terminal building where Brad picked her up. They drove to Skamania Lodge, had a couples' massage followed by an early, long, and delicious dinner, and an even longer and more delicious round of lovemaking.

The following morning, she asked about places to hike, pretending she knew nothing about the geography of the area. He immediately suggested Beacon Rock, the 848-foot massive basalt column west of the resort, which once formed the core of an ancient volcano. The route to the top of Beacon Rock covers nearly a mile of switchbacks on a sheer rock wall. Getting to the top on most summer days is like snaking around in line for a Disneyland ride, there are so many people on the trail. But this Sunday, early in the morning, they were alone as they began the gentle walk through the forest at the base to get to the southernmost face of the rock.

It's not a technical climb, more like a walk up a steep path on a trail marked with ironwork bridges and steps. It was a gorgeous day, and they stopped at every overlook to see the river beneath them and the scenery around them. Not to mention to let their lungs catch up with their muscle exertions. This time, the breathlessness when she was with Brad wasn't from his kisses, which was a first.

Claudia was smiling when they reached the summit. Part of it was being happy to have reached the top. Part was being there with him. Part was a sudden memory of a story she knew, which always made her smile and want to whirl around in a *Sound of*

Music moment. Brad caught her expression before she could tamp it down. "What's the secret look about, lovely?"

"No secret. I'm happy to be at the top, that's all."

"I may not have known you long, but I know that smile means something else. Don't want to tell me?"

"Well, I guess I can." She laughed at what she imagined the expression on her friend Ruth's face would be if she knew Claudia was about to spill her secret. "I have a friend ..."

"Is this one of those stories that's actually about you but you're too embarrassed to admit it?"

"No, it really is about a friend. I've been sworn to secrecy and can't reveal her name ..."

"Or she'd have to kill you."

"Something like that. But you have to stop interrupting so I can tell you the story."

With his thumb and forefinger, he made a zipping motion across his mouth, although the imaginary zipper didn't stop a grin from appearing.

"Anyway, this friend had a boyfriend—they eventually got married and now have a baby daughter, which is the reason this story can't get out. At least until the daughter is, like, thirty."

Her friend had called her in a panic when she realized someday her daughter might hear this story. "So, right after they got engaged, my friend and her guy came here. It was the first spring weekend with really clear weather. They got here early and were the only people on the rock. When they got to the top, he kissed her and whispered, 'Hooray, hooray, it's the first of May.' She finished with 'outdoor screwing begins today,' and he asked her if she was game. She said yes and they did."

Brad pulled her to him, kissed her, and said, "It's not the first of May, but I'm game if you are."

"No, no," she said, sure panic had made an unwanted appearance in her voice. "I didn't mean I wanted to ..."

He laughed. "Actually, I didn't either. I'm too used to a nice comfortable bed. We should be someplace private, intimate, not in public with kids and dogs around." He motioned to the group coming up behind them—a mother and father, two high-school-age daughters, and a golden retriever.

They looked vaguely familiar; at least the two young daughters did, although she couldn't figure out why. Brad definitely knew them, if the smile he was directing to them was any indication.

"Well, I'll be damned. Hello, Turners. Nice day for a hike, isn't it?" He extended his hand to the man who was smiling in return. When the handshake was over, he turned to her. "This is Janet and Jim Turner, Claire. And these two are Julie and Jessica. They're two of my students at St. Mary's. This is my friend, Claire Mason."

Another round of handshakes while Claire tried to figure out if she knew them and, if she did, whether she should jump off Beacon Rock to change the subject and hope for the best. There was something about the family that tickled at her memory, but she couldn't put her finger on it.

Her worst fears were realized when Janet, the mother, said, "You look familiar, although I don't recognize your name. Any chance I know you?"

"I doubt it," Brad said. "She's from Seattle."

Janet persisted. "I'm sure I've met you."

Brad looked at her, a questioning look in his eyes. She knew what he was asking, but she was not going to reveal her April Mayes persona to a family of strangers. "I can't imagine we've met unless you've been in one of my classes. I teach English lit at Bellevue College."

Janet said, "That's not it. We do have a daughter who's an English major in college, but she goes to Portland State."

Crap. Crap. Crap. Now she knew why they looked familiar. She'd had a student last year named Jocelyn Turner who was obviously a member of this family.

Janet continued, "You're a teacher like Brad. Do you write romances, too?"

Her husband rolled his eyes. "She has dozens of romance novels on her Kindle, including all of yours, Brad. It's not enough we shovel money at St. Mary's to pay your salary, but we subsidize your afterhours job, too."

Panicked at how to turn the conversation away from her, Claudia grabbed at the first thing she could think of. "Brad's a good writer, isn't he? What's your favorite of his books?" Brad looked disappointed she wasn't telling the Turners about her other life. But at least this lie was one of omission.

"Oh, I always seem to like the most recent one the best," Janet said.

"I think *Mrs. Duniway's Assistant* is terrific, too," Claudia responded. "I recently read it myself."

When the conversation died after her compliment on his book, Brad stepped in. "We'll let you savor your moment at the top. We're on our way down so I can get Claire to the airport for her plane back to Seattle. Nice to see you, Turners. See you two," he winked at the young girls, "on Monday. And I don't want any I-was-stranded-on-a-mountain excuses for not doing your homework assignment."

One of the twins, Claudia wasn't sure which one, giggled. "We had to have it all finished before we left home this morning. Don't worry."

"Good. Then enjoy the rest of the day."

They didn't talk on the way down to the car. When they were all buckled in and she expected him to start the car, he didn't. Instead, he stared out the windshield for a few moments before saying, "Why didn't you want the Turners to know you write romance novels? You're a great writer. You shouldn't be ashamed of your work."

"How do you know what kind of writer I am? I thought you'd never read anything I wrote."

"I hadn't when we talked at the conference. I bought *The Storm Inside* when I got home. I finally had time to start it last week. I'm not finished yet, but what I've read so far is beautifully written. Based on *The Tempest*, isn't it?"

"Thank you. And, yes, it is. That's one of my favorite Shakespeare plays. When were you going to tell me you read it?"

"It's one of my favorite plays, too. And I thought I'd wait until after I finished it to tell you how much I enjoyed it." He glanced over at her. "But you're changing the subject. Why not tell the Turners about your work? They can't do your career in Seattle any harm."

"Maybe. Maybe not. Anyway, I'm so used to keeping it secret I'm not comfortable letting anyone know. Particular strangers."

"They're not strangers. They're friends."

"Of yours. Not mine. I can't take the chance until after the tenure committee meets. Why do you think I'm so careful about being seen with you? I told you, two of the committee members have very strange ideas about commercial fiction. Even yours, I imagine." She wanted him to understand it wasn't going to happen until she felt safe from her colleagues' disdain. It would help if she could tell him about her connection with the Turners' daughter and her fear that the news of her extracurricular activities would get back to her colleagues through them, but she couldn't.

"And when does the committee make a decision?"

"In six weeks."

He shook his head, started the car, and put it in gear. "I guess I can hold out until then. But I have to tell you, I'm at the point where I want to stand on top of Beacon Rock and shout how happy I am because of the beautiful woman I'm involved with." He pulled out onto Highway 14 and headed west.

"Is that what we are? Involved? I've wondered."

"What the hell did you think we were? The world's longest one-night stand?"

Chapter 11

Even after a second weekend in Seattle, Brad was still mystified by the lovely Claire. Unlike every other woman he'd been involved with, she was more fascinating the longer they were together. The more time he spent with her, the more he wanted to be with her.

But he couldn't shake the feeling there was something going on with her. He was sure she was keeping a secret from him, but he couldn't imagine what it could be. And he was no closer to figuring it out after four weekends than he had been after one.

He thought they'd talked about everything. From their academic careers and writing to politics both in their jobs and on the national level to the minutia of which vegetables they loved and hated. They'd exchanged childhood memories and were amused to discover both had had dogs named Spot when they were kids and they both disliked seeing animals dressed in costumes.

They'd even gotten into the deep stuff. On the last weekend they were together at her place in Seattle, they'd talked about families. He had told her all about his dysfunctional family of five children and two completely irresponsible, immature parents who he loved but who he really didn't think should have been allowed to be responsible for a goldfish let alone five kids. He'd picked out a few funny stories about their notoriously careless parenting to share, like how they had once argued with a teacher about his sister's work only to find out the teacher had one of his brothers in the class. He assured her that somehow, all his siblings had survived without anyone being jailed or permanently disabled, although it had been close in a couple of instances, including several scrapes he'd had with the authorities when he was a teen. For the first time, he told someone about his juvenile record and how, if it ever came out he'd been picked up for shoplifting once and vandalism more than once, he could lose his job. He counted on the fact that juvie records were sealed at eighteen if there are no further problems. There hadn't been, but he still worried. He even told her he'd lied about it when he'd applied at St. Mary's. He had justified the lie at the time by telling himself he'd been asked if he'd ever been convicted of a felony and he'd only committed misdemeanors, but he knew he was on shaky ground.

He didn't tell her how much he had resented his parents for showing little interest in their children or how they made promise after promise, not one of which was kept. The promise to pick him up at a friend's house but never show. The promise to buy a special present for his birthday but somehow lose track of when the big day was and get the gift to him weeks later. Or never. The lie about how much they loved their kids when clearly they really only cared for each other. At least, it's how they came across to their children.

Claire told him a bit about her family, mostly about her father, who'd died when she was in undergraduate school. She had been the light of his life, it sounded like, and she missed him still. When Brad prodded a bit, she admitted she had a "baby" brother and a mother, neither of whom were close to her. Her brother was lost in the bottom of a bottle someplace in LA, and she hadn't seen him in over ten years. Her mother lived in a cabin in the woods someplace in Colorado, and although there were sporadic phone calls between the two, they hadn't been together in more than two years. Her mother had always favored her brother and had gone into hiding, almost, when he had disappeared. Her daughter's achievements were a footnote to her mother, much to Claire's dismay.

Her story made him understand better her drive to succeed in her career and why the regard of her colleagues and achieving tenure were both so important to her.

Neither of them, they agreed, had come from a family that would have won awards from *Parents Magazine*, although Brad was glad he had his parents rather than hers. At least he and all his siblings loved each other even if they had not exactly been tended to with care. They'd always had each other's backs as they stumbled their way through the maze of growing up.

Claire had overcome considerably more hurdles than he had in both her academic and professional lives—a testament to the strength of her character, he told her. She brushed it off, but the smile she tried hard to hide when he gave her the compliment said she appreciated it.

The smile disappeared when he asked her if she planned on seeing her mom when she went to Denver for the Romance Writers of America conference. She not only said she wasn't planning to call her mom but backpedaled about going to the meeting at all. He tried to encourage her to attend, but she closed up; she said she would make up her mind about it soon. He wasn't sure if she was resisting because her mother lived in Colorado, because she didn't want to go to any more writers' conferences, or because of something he'd done. He let the subject drop and moved on to asking how her writing was going.

But something about their conversation had apparently triggered a reaction from Claire, and not a good one. In their texts and phone conversations, she began to make excuses about why she might not be able to go to RWA, in spite of her earlier plans to attend. She also began to take longer to respond to him.

Finally, he sent a text that seemed to get her attention.

What have I done to piss you off? Please tell me so I don't do it again.

She responded right away.

Nothing. It's me. I'm struggling with my book. Please forgive.

He wrote back:

It's not me, it's you? LOL. Can I see you next weekend?

He wasn't happy with her response:

I'm booked. Not sure when the next open weekend is.

This was not good. She'd always been as eager to see him as he was to see her. Whatever was eating at her must be serious. He had to find out what it was. Figuring he had nothing to lose, he pushed back.

What about RWA? We're still meeting in Denver, aren't we?

When there was no response for hours, he was sure he'd blown it. The "nothing to lose" attitude had, in fact, lost him something important—Claire. He was sure she'd given up on their relationship.

Then, unexpectedly, he got an answer.

Okay, I'll meet you in Denver.

He'd wanted to coordinate their flights, but he didn't press his luck by insisting. He texted back:

What day are you arriving?

Her response came an hour later.

Mary Lynn and I are booked on a flight arriving late in the afternoon of the first day. We're sharing a room in the convention hotel.

Sharing a room with her agent? Definitely a crimp in his plans to have her with him the whole time they were in Denver. He wasn't sure if Mary Lynn knew about them or, if she did know, if she'd approve of Claire spending the night in his room. What the hell was going on?

Chapter 12

"You don't have to inspect my suitcase, Mary Lynn. All the trampy clothes and hooker heels from the last conference I went to are there along with enough makeup for the cast of a major Broadway musical. I didn't forget anything." Claudia had come back to her agent's home after her hair and nails appointment to find Mary Lynn digging into her suitcase.

"I didn't think you had. I was tucking a little surprise in your belongings for you to find when we got to Denver." She pulled an envelope out of the side pocket of the suitcase and handed it to Claudia. "But now that I got caught, I'll give it to you here."

Claudia opened the envelope. Inside was a contract for her next four books. "Four books? I thought we were only going to get a two-book contract?"

"'Thank you for being the best agent an author could have,' might be the better response, don't you think?"

Claudia grinned. "Yes. It would. And I'm sorry. You *are* the best agent an author could have. Thank you. But how ...?"

"Your sales have been great, out the roof since San Fran, which pleased them. You won those awards this year and, I hear, might pick up another one in Denver. Your last book just hit number one on the *USA Today* list, and the two before were on Amazon's top ten list for weeks. You're an overachiever. Tom was happy you've started showing up at conferences but is now worried you'll meet a publisher you like better at one of them and leave him. Or, God help us, go indie and self-pub, since you have such a loyal following. So he decided to tie you up, so to speak, all for himself."

"Why would he think I want to leave? I've been happy with him."

Mary Lynn's cat-with-canary-feathers-sticking-out-of-her-smile was the tell.

"Oh, my God, you told him I was looking at other options."

"I may have indicated something of that nature. Perhaps hinted at the other publishers who've been sniffing around you for a while."

"You lied to him?"

"Nope. I didn't have to lie. There *have* been other publishers sniffing around you, or at least asking questions about whether you're happy where you are. I merely let Tom know of their existence."

"Well, whatever you did, thank you. I'm thrilled. Four books! What's the timeline?"

"Two a year, like always. You'll have plenty of time to get them done."

"You are the best, Mary Lynn."

"Yes, I know. Now, let's get to the airport. Alaska Airlines waits for no man. Or woman—not even the Queen of Steam."

• • •

If Romancing the Writer had turned the St. Francis Hotel into a beehive, the Romance Writers of America convention made the conference hotel in Denver look like all the remaining bees in the world had gathered in one place where they buzzed around, generating noise and energy at a level Claudia had never heard before. In the lobby, women—again, almost all the attendees were female—greeted each other like long-lost sisters, shrieks of pleasure, yelps of surprise, and cries of recognition blending into a cacophony of sound. Not usually intimidated by crowds, Claudia was cowed into silence by the sheer number of people around her. Mary Lynn had gone to get their room and convention registrations, leaving her client to sit on a large overstuffed couch, big-eyed, watching the chaos around her.

The size of the convention had never even occurred to her. It certainly did now. There were hundreds of people in the lobby. She'd have to be more on her toes here than she'd been in San Francisco. There were simply more people to worry about. More chances one of them might actually know her in her other life; recognize her in spite of her "disguise." Why in the world had she thought she could keep pulling off this charade? She had so many details to keep straight about who she was supposed to be in various settings, she had to think hard to remember which person she was before she spoke to anyone. She'd even screwed up her registration for the convention, putting her return address as Mary Lynn's in Seattle because she'd been obsessing about how she was going to deal with Brad at the conference while she filled out the form.

The longer she sat waiting for her agent to return with their room key, the more nervous she became. She was on the verge of making a run for the exit when a familiar male voice broke her concentration. Brad. She was now officially and completely freaked out.

"I can't believe I found you in this crowd. It must be a sign." Brad sat down next to her on the couch. "I've missed you, lovely." She noticed he was careful not to sit too close or to touch her, for which she was grateful. It was hard enough maintaining her April Mayes persona when she was with Mary Lynn, let alone when he was in the mix. She quickly scanned the lobby hoping no one was watching—at least, no one who could identify either one of them.

"Brad. Nice to see you. Have you checked in yet?"

She knew from the way he pulled back he was disappointed by her response. He sounded confused when he responded. "Ah, yes, I have. I was ... I mean ... I saw you sitting here and ... are you all settled?"

"Mary Lynn's taking care of it now." She stood and he did, too. "I better go find her. I'd like to freshen up." She started toward the registration desk, but he touched her arm, stopping her.

"I came over to ask if we can have dinner tonight. Please?"

"I'll have to check with Mary Lynn, but if she's free, it might work."

"I meant you and me. Without a chaperone."

"Oh, well, I'm not sure." She tried to pull away, but his hold tightened. "I hate to leave her stranded all by herself in a strange city."

"She's surrounded by hundreds of people, half of whom she knows, I'm sure, Claire."

"Please, while we're here, will you use my pen name? That's what my name tag will say and what everyone thinks is my name."

"All right, then, *April.*" He rubbed his hand over his face and sighed. "Look, I don't know what happened between our last weekend in Seattle and now, but I have to find out. You can't shut me out this way. Not after ..."

She shook her head so hard she swore she could feel the extensions trying to escape. "I'm not shutting you out. I'm distracted by work and the crowd and ..."

"Then have dinner with me. Mary Lynn will understand, won't she?"

"Mary Lynn will understand about what, Brad?" Claudia hadn't heard or seen her agent approach them. Not a good sign. She had to be on her toes the whole four days, and this was so not a good start.

Brad held out his hand, and Mary Lynn shook it. "I asked Claire ... ah, April ... to have dinner with me, and she put me off until she talked to you. You won't mind if we sneak off someplace, will you?"

"Not if I have a chance to follow up with you on the phone conversation we had a couple weeks ago. You never got back to me. I may have an interesting opportunity for you."

"Done. How about all three of us have coffee in the morning before the sessions start, assuming you don't mind talking in front of April?"

"Not at all. And early morning is perfect. I have pitch appointments all day beginning at nine, but before then, I'm free." She handed Claudia a key card. "We're in room 1019. I'll go on up, and you can ..."

"I'm coming with you." Claudia pulled the handle out of her suitcase and turned to follow her agent.

"About dinner tonight," Brad said. "How about meeting here at six thirty? I'll find a place for us to eat and arrange for transportation to get us there. That work?"

"Yes, sure. Fine." Before he could make her life any more complicated, she made for the elevator as though her butt was on fire.

• • •

"What the hell was that all about? You acted like Brad was a perfect stranger. Grant you he is pretty perfect but not so much a stranger, if our conversations of the past six weeks are correct. Why are you acting so standoffish?"

Claudia hadn't even shut the door to their shared room before Mary Lynn began her questions.

She shook her head and said nothing.

"If you think I'm going to give up asking, you don't really know me. He has it bad for you. Any fool can see that. Why are you pushing him away?"

"I don't know what you think you're seeing but he can't 'have it bad' for me. He doesn't even know who I am. He thinks I'm some hot romance writer who hides behind a pen name to protect her career at Bellevue College. He thinks I live in Seattle. Hell, he even thinks I like those horrible cabbage rose slipcovers you have on your furniture."

"And whose fault is that—not the slipcovers. I claim them. The other stuff."

"Mine, of course. Although you helped. I'm beginning to feel guilty every time I look at him because the only true thing in the whole list of what I've told him is I hide behind a pen name. The rest is all lies, including—maybe especially—the fake name I gave him to avoid giving him my real name when he knew I used a pen name. Oh, hell, I can't even keep it all straight anymore." Her throat began to feel thick and choked, like she was going to cry. The last time she'd cried about a man was when her father died. It had been snotty and ugly, with red eyes and a swollen face, and she'd vowed never to repeat it.

"You don't think in the past six weeks, he's been able to see the truth of who you are, whatever name he thinks you go by?"

"How can he? I've lied about everything."

"So you keep saying. But he's a smart guy. I think he knows full well who he loves."

"Loves? Are you crazy? We're having a good time, nothing more."

"Yeah, which explains why you're on the verge of crying while you rip at your cuticles in the room you insisted we share so you wouldn't have the temptation to spend the whole conference in his room."

Claudia stopped picking at her fingers, a bad habit she thought she'd lost years ago. Trust a man to bring it back to the surface. "I thought it would be fun to share a room with you. It had nothing to do with him. He's just a ... I don't know ... maybe just a friend. Or something."

Mary Lynn put her arms around her client. "Girlfriend, he is so much more than a friend. You may not want to face it, but you're in love with Brad Davis. Like he is with you. For God's sake, something this good comes along so rarely, why would you even think about letting it pass you by?"

"How can love be built on lies?"

"It can't. So you have to tell him the truth."

Claudia dropped onto the sofa in the living area. "I want to, but it's never been the right time."

"When would the right time be, I wonder? When you're applying for a marriage license and have to show ID? For God's sake, tell him the truth about yourself. At dinner tonight, maybe. He's a teacher. He'll understand your need to protect your professional reputation, won't he?"

"He's said a couple of times how careful he is with his. Maybe you're right. Maybe he would understand."

"Then do it. Tell him. Tonight."

•••

Brad paced the confines of his room, trying to figure out what the hell had happened between the last weekend he'd spent with Claire and their recent encounter in the hotel lobby. It had been less than ten days between the two but a gap of monumental proportions seemed to have opened between them.

Ever since their second weekend together, when they'd worked so productively at the coast, bouncing ideas off each other, laughing at the weird things autocorrect did with slightly misspelled words in a love scene (Claire's problem) and the archaic words in an historical novel (his problem), their compatibility had been obvious, not to mention their chemistry. It only took a couple more weekends for him to believe firmly and absolutely that she was the one he'd thought he'd never find. She was smart, talented, beautiful, and funny. She made him both laugh and think. She made his blood heat with only a glance, and when they were in bed, she burned up the sheets with her passion. She was a match for him everywhere.

They shared both a vocation and an avocation. They even had some similarity in their backgrounds. What more could a man want? The only problem was she seemed to be holding something back from him. He assumed it had something to do with her writing, since her academic career seemed an open book. Maybe it was how much money she made. Maybe she thought he wouldn't like someone making more money than he did. He'd seen her books on the bestseller lists, so he knew she was more successful, commercially, than he was. It didn't bother him in the least. He was proud to know someone who wrote as well and successfully as she did. He'd read another of her books recently and recognized the inspiration—*Brains and Brawn* was loosely based on *Sense and Sensibility*—and he'd loved both the story and the fact he knew the author. Intimately.

He was sure she'd be granted tenure when the committee met in a few weeks and hoped then she'd have the nerve to go public. Everyone, especially her colleagues, needed both to know how skillful a writer she was and to appreciate her talent as much as he did.

After a quick shower and shave, he dressed as carefully for their dinner date as he had for his job interview at St. Mary's—black suit, white shirt with no tie, his favorite cuff links. He splashed on some aftershave she'd once said she liked, checked his nails to make sure they were clean and clipped, his teeth to make sure there was nothing weird hiding there. He was the picture of sartorial and well-groomed splendor.

And he was ready an hour before they were to meet. So he went down to the lobby to have a different space in which to pace and worry about how, if the evening didn't work out, he'd have seen the end of the best relationship he'd had with a woman in years. Maybe in forever.

He'd made reservations at the Briarwood Inn, a restaurant a colleague of his had suggested as one of the best and most romantic in the area. He hoped it worked to make things easy between them. He needed all the help he could get.

Thoughts of Claire had been driving him crazy all afternoon. Now it was the sight of her walking across the lobby toward him that did it. She was in an electric blue, body-hugging dress, which seemed modest enough—everything was covered quite completely—but which clung to every single curve on her body. Her beautiful breasts were out of sight, not even a hint of cleavage showing, but he knew what lay beneath the fabric that seemed to lovingly hug them, as he'd like to do. Her hips, too, were encased in bright blue, and when she walked, he could see them shift as well as see the outline of her legs in April's hooker heels press against the skirt, one at a time, as she made her way toward him. Jesus, he was getting a hard-on watching her.

And so, he was sure, were the few men who were in the lobby and who were doing everything but drooling as she took her time getting over to him. He couldn't stand it any longer and strode to reach her before some other man made a claim on her.

Boldly, he kissed her cheek and inhaled the familiar scent of her. He had never asked her what the name of her perfume was; he was sure no woman he knew had worn it. He knew he'd forever think of her if he smelled it again.

"Hello, lovely. You look beautiful tonight." When he pulled back from the kiss, he frowned a little. "How did you grow your hair back so fast? It hasn't been long enough since I've seen you for it to get so much longer. And it's redder than it was the last time, too."

"You've apparently never heard of hair extensions. Mary Lynn thinks I need to have long, flowing hair to look like a sexy romance writer." She flipped a strand or two back from her face. "And redheads are in right now so I have a henna rinse put on it."

He took the coat she had over her arm and draped it over her shoulders. "You'd look sexy with your head shaved or dyed bright orange, I imagine, especially in the dress you're wearing." Taking her elbow, he continued. "In fact, I need to get you out of here before one of the other men standing around here who have been lusting after you challenges me to a duel at sunrise for you. I have a cab ordered. It should be outside waiting."

She laughed. "You're exaggerating, but thank you for the compliment."

Good. She sounded like she was back to the Claire he knew from their weekends together. Maybe everything would turn out all right after all.

Chapter 13

Claudia was doing her best to be relaxed and comfortable with Brad. God knows, he was trying to make it easy for her. He'd complimented her profusely when they met in the lobby. He had picked a wonderful place for their dinner. He'd ordered champagne and made a lovely toast when it was poured for them. Knowing she had decided to tell him the truth about her name and her life, however, made her tense in spite of his efforts. She had hoped the wine would help, but it seemed to disappear fast without making her feel any looser. Much more of it, and she was afraid she'd go from tense to tipsy without passing relaxed.

After they ordered their dinner, Brad sat back in his chair and watched her for a few moments, long enough to make her uneasy about what he might be about to say. Finally, he said, "How are you doing? You've seemed maybe worried lately. Tense, certainly. I'm told I'm a good listener if you want to unload on me."

She could feel the tension begin to curl around in her stomach again like some kind of angry snake. She took another sip of wine to see if she could send the beast back where it belonged. Then she had an idea of how to broach the subject of her lies. She eased into it with, "I've been frantic at work. There's getting everything in order for the tenure committee, and a couple students I've been working with who've been giving me trouble." She played with the tableware in front of her. "The worst part is my book is stalled. I can't seem to get my hero and heroine on the same page. Or should I say, in the same chapter. They keep wandering off in different directions. They don't seem to want to talk to each other."

He laughed. "I hate it when my characters won't do what I want them to do. Although, I guess I should be grateful my subconscious usually knows them well enough to prod me in the direction their personalities would take them."

"Is that what happens? I was beginning to believe characters were bitchy people who live to torment a writer until she gives in and lets them run amok."

He leaned in, his forearms on the table. "Tell me what they're doing—or not doing. Maybe I can help."

Here goes. Let's see how he takes this. "Well, the heroine has been keeping something from the hero about who she is. That's why she's avoiding him. Her father and his are old enemies, and she's sure if the hero finds out, he won't love her. I can't find a way to get the truth told without having a huge confrontation before I'm ready for one."

"Hmm. I see your problem. Sounds like this one is a take on *Romeo and Juliet.*"

"Yes, and with a happier ending. Do you think he's more likely to be angry about who she is or about the fact she's been hiding the truth?"

"Definitely the lying. That's a deal-breaker for me, anyway. I had a relationship fall apart because the woman I was seeing lied to me. She failed to tell me she was married when we started seeing each other—separated but still married—to a husband who wanted her back. The time we ran into him in a restaurant wasn't pleasant." He hesitated as if there was more but said nothing else.

"Did it get ugly?"

"No, because I wouldn't let it. We didn't see each other after that evening. I never called her again. Didn't much appreciate being in the dark about details like a husband. Then there was the divorced colleague who never told any of us she had three kids because she wanted to appear to be carefree. Who the hell would lie about their own kids? I think she was interested in getting to know me better, but I couldn't see it." He took a sip of his wine. "I mean, if she lied about her kids, what else would she lie about?"

Their entrees arrived, and they set about eating them, leaving Claudia to think way too much about what he'd said while she tried to swallow her steak without choking. Whether it was on the meat or on his stories, she wasn't sure.

As they were eating dessert, he returned to the subject, much to her discomfort. "To get back to your misbehaving characters, what have you tried so far to sort it out?"

"Well, I tried having her tell him when they were having dinner, but she couldn't find a way to raise the subject. Then I thought about having her write an e-mail ..."

"Too impersonal. Text is even worse. Phone call might not even work."

"That's what I decided, too, at least about the e-mail and text. I still might try a phone call if the scene I have in mind doesn't grab me when I write it next week."

"What's your idea for the scene?"

"I think I'll have her tell him when they're in bed. You know, in the afterglow of great sex. But I haven't quite figured out what his reaction will be. Which is why I haven't written it yet."

He laughed. "Tell him after hot sex! There speaks the Queen of Steam! Now that I think about it, it might work. All those endorphins from good sex do make a guy mellow. Although isn't he likely to drift off to sleep right afterward and miss what she's saying?"

"My heroes always stay awake long enough to cuddle."

"Which is why it's fiction." He grinned. "Although if he does fall asleep while she's telling him, it would give you another layer of complication. She thinks she told him. He swears she didn't."

"I'll have to think about it, I guess." She offered him a spoonful of her chocolate mousse. "Here, you absolutely have to taste this. It's spectacular."

She made sure there was no more talk about her book at dinner. But she did tuck away the idea of telling him when they were in bed, assuming that's where they were headed after dinner. It could be her best chance to tell him when he was relaxed after they'd had their usual spectacular sex.

During the cab ride from the restaurant, she asked about the progress on his book about race relations in Oregon featuring the story of Dr. DeNorval Unthank, the first black doctor in the state. From his response to her question, it was obvious he was pleased with his progress. In fact, the entire cab ride back to the hotel was happily taken up with his explanation.

Claudia had never been so content to be on the receiving end of a lecture about someone else's book.

• • •

By the time they reached their hotel, the cabbie could have written the book Brad was working on, he had told Claire so much about it. She'd asked a couple questions he hadn't thought of, which made him pull out the small notebook and pen he always carried so he could jot down ideas. Talking about their work was one of the things he loved about their relationship. He'd never had this kind of give-and-take with another woman before.

They seemed, over the course of the evening, to have gotten back on firm ground, and he couldn't be happier. Mere happiness turned to elation when he asked her if she wanted a nightcap in the bar, and she'd said she'd rather have it in his room. He got her in the elevator and on the way up to his floor before she had even a moment to reconsider.

They had barely made it into his room when she damn near attacked him. Well, not really. But she sure as hell stopped him cold two steps into the room with a scorching hot kiss that had their tongues tangling and his dick hardening, eager to come out to join the party. Before he could move, she slipped his jacket off his shoulders and began to unbutton his shirt.

"I've wanted to do this all evening," she said. "You look so hot. You smell so good. I'd say you set out to seduce me tonight."

"And I can't tell you how glad I am to see it's working."

She pressed her hips into his, rubbing against his erection. "I can tell you're happy."

He ran his hands down her back looking for a way to get her out of her dress. "How the hell do I get this thing off you? I can't find a zipper."

She laughed and moved his hand to her left side. "It's here. Then it comes off over my head."

What was in front of him when he followed her instructions took his breath away. He swore she was wearing nothing but three patches of black lace, two barely covering her nipples, one struggling to contain her mound. "Jesus, woman, who had plans to seduce whom?"

She stepped over the dress he'd let drop to the floor and said, "I love a man who knows the difference between *who* and *whom*." She tugged at his shirttails to get them out of his pants. "This needs to come off. I want to see that beautiful chest of yours."

He obliged. She then tugged at the buckle on his belt. "The pants, too, lover."

After he took a condom from his pants pocket, he stripped down, then backed her to the edge of the bed the housekeeping staff had conveniently turned down for them. She hopped up and lay back on the pillows, one leg bent with the knee in the air, the other flat. When she put her hands behind her head, she looked like she was hanging out, relaxing. But the flush on her cheeks and her ragged breathing said she was anything but at ease.

He joined her in bed, kneeling beside her, and cradled her face in his hands. "You are the most beautiful thing I've ever seen. Ever imagined. I'm so glad you're here tonight. I've been worried ..."

"Shh. Not now. Later." With her hands at the back of his neck, she pulled his mouth to hers, urging him to open for her, sliding her tongue past his lips when he did.

Someone moaned. He wasn't sure which one of them. He didn't care. All he wanted was to taste more of her body. He slid a slender, silken strap off one shoulder and caressed the breast he found under the bit of lace it was attached to. Then he did the same with the second strap. When he discovered the tiny bow between her breasts that released the whole thing, he untied it and feasted on the best gift he'd ever unwrapped.

From the restless way she was moving, and the little sounds he knew she made when she was on her way to an orgasm, he knew she was ready for him, wanted him to enter her. But he wasn't yet ready to give up exploring more of her body, eager as he was to reacquaint his mouth and his hands with every glorious inch of her.

He trailed kisses down her neck and then to her breasts. His hand slid along her ribs to the spot between her legs he knew would be hot and wet for him. She clenched her thighs around his hand, as if to keep it from leaving. As if he would. But the last patch of lace was in the way. He ripped at it, and it disappeared.

As he suckled at her breast, he entered her with one finger, then two, rubbing the tight bundle of nerves at the apex of her sex. He could feel her legs begin to tremble, heard her breath catch, and knew she was close. Her body bowed toward him, and she called his name. As she came down from the orgasm, he sheathed himself in the condom and entered her with one strong thrust.

Heaven. He'd entered heaven.

• • •

Claudia held tight to Brad's shoulders and felt a second climax begin, her inner muscles growing tight around his penis. He hooked an arm behind one knee and angled her body up so he could thrust deeper into her. He filled her completely; every empty space in her body seemed full of Brad. As the orgasm hit her with a force like a hurricane, with one final thrust and calling "Claire. Oh, God, Claire," Brad reached his climax, too.

He collapsed on her, buried his head in her neck, nipped at her jaw, then began to move off. But she held him in place, needing to feel the weight of him on her. Needing his strong body against hers. Still.

After a few minutes of complete silence, broken only by the sounds of their mutual attempts to get their ragged breathing under control, he rolled to his side, taking her with him, still in his strong arms, still inside her. He kissed the tip of her nose. "You are the most amazing woman I've ever known."

"You're pretty amazing yourself," was all she could think of to say.

"I need to go take care of this condom. Want anything while I'm up?"

"No, I'm fine." *I'm not fine because I'm about to tell you something that'll make you hate me, but I have to do it.*

He wasn't gone long. He returned with a warm, wet washcloth so she could clean herself up a bit. It was what he always did, but this time, his thoughtfulness made her want to cry because she was going to ruin the whole evening with what she told him, she was sure.

Also as he always did, he spooned around her when he got back in bed. Between yawns, he asked, "Can you spend the night, or does Mary Lynn expect you back in your room?"

"I'll leave in a little bit. She probably doesn't care but ... well, you know."

"Yup. I know. Your reputation." Yawns again.

Not seeing him made it a bit easier to say what she wanted to say. So she started. "You know the conversation we had about my heroine having something she's hidden from my hero?"

"Mm. At dinner. Sure."

"Well, it's one of those things I wrote from real life, I'm afraid. There's something I need to tell you."

His breathing was becoming shallow and even.

"Brad? Are you awake?"

"Mmm. How could I fall asleep when you're telling me something about your book?"

"Not my book. About me. I've been ..."

"If I was the guy you're writing about, I'd be furious if the woman I loved lied to me. Nothing worse than lying parents and lying lovers."

Her breathing caught, and she swore her heart skipped a beat. Maybe two or three. She didn't know what to do. Should she plunge ahead and tell him anyway? And what did he mean, lying parents?

"Brad?"

There was no answer. She shifted a bit so she was out from the circle of his arms. It was obvious when he didn't pull her back against him that he was definitely asleep.

"Oh, Brad. I want to tell you the truth so badly but I'm afraid you'll hate me. And I don't know what's worse—lying to you and keeping you or telling the truth and losing you. I think I'm in love with you."

"Love with you, too," came from the sleeping man next to her.

She slipped out of bed, gathered up her clothes and shoes, and headed for the bathroom. She'd never believed in hell up until this very moment. Now she knew it was real.

<h1 style="text-align:center">Chapter 14</h1>

Mary Lynn was sound asleep when Claudia got back to their room. And thanks to the note Claudia left before she crawled into her bed, her agent went to the breakfast meeting with Brad the next morning alone. Claudia didn't leave the room all morning, didn't even dress, knowing Mary Lynn was booked with appointments and wouldn't be back. She intended to stay put until she figured out a way to face Brad and tell him the truth. Or until hell froze over. Which one was likely to occur first, she wasn't sure.

Then she remembered the book signing that afternoon. She was slated to be there, in the same space with Brad. Although with any luck, not next to him again. Reluctantly, she showered and began to dress.

The perplexing part of her conversations with Brad the night before was, somehow, she felt as if she *had* told him about her fake identity by cloaking it as a plot problem and he hadn't understood it. In her head, she knew she'd done no such thing. But somehow, the devil on her shoulder kept saying she'd dropped enough breadcrumbs to lead him to the right conclusion. The resulting confusion left her feeling guilty for not telling him, fearful of what he'd say if he did follow the breadcrumbs, and a tiny bit of relief he hadn't even if she was disappointed he hadn't been astute enough to figure it out. She was so confused by her own reactions, it was no wonder she couldn't figure out how to confront Brad.

She still hadn't come to a conclusion by the time she was due in the ballroom for the author signing. So she finished putting on her April Mayes clothes, face, and shoes and mentally prepared herself for a possibly embarrassing and very public scene if Brad had seen the light and understood she was hiding something from him. If he demanded to know what it was while they were in public, she wasn't sure what she'd say.

Mary Lynn was already at the table assigned to her, unpacking books. Her sly grin was enough to set Claudia's teeth on edge. "Good night last night, was it? I didn't hear you come in, and you were sleeping so soundly this morning I don't think an earthquake could have disturbed you."

"Can we get this table set up and skip the small talk?"

Mary Lynn fussed with an arrangement of postcards and bookmarks as she continued, ignoring Claudia's suggestion. "Brad seemed very happy this morning, although he was disappointed you weren't at our meeting. I told him you'd gotten in late, and he grinned like a silly fool."

Maybe a change of subject would get her agent off the topic of the night before. "Did breakfast go well? Are you signing him as a new client?"

"It looks that way. You don't mind, do you?"

"Why should I?"

"You seem to have developed a proprietary interest in him over the past weeks."

"I don't own him. And you're the best agent I know." She slapped a book on top of a pile of others, realized it was not the right one, and slung it back into the box behind the table.

Mary Lynn frowned at her. "Something's off here. What's going on? He's happy. You're not. I expected it would be the other way around after you told him ..."

"I didn't tell him."

"Aha. Now I understand. Why the hell not?"

"It never seemed the right time to bring it up."

"I can't imagine how that could happen. I mean, don't all your conversations with the men you love include some discussion of how you're hiding behind not one but two fake names, a fake phone number, and carrying on in someone else's home, which you claim as yours?"

"Sarcasm duly noted, as well as the repetition of what you have already lectured me about." Claudia rearranged the books on the table, trying to avoid Mary Lynn's gaze. "And I don't love him. I don't think I do, anyway." She dropped into the chair and gave up pretending to arrange her display. "Okay, maybe I do, but I've never told him." *As long as you don't count saying it when he's asleep and I'm trying to get out of his room as fast as I can.*

"Look, I tried to tell him. I really did. But when I sort of broached the subject, he made it clear how much he hated being lied to. I chickened out. I'll have to find another way to handle this."

"Handle what, lovely?" Brad asked, coming up behind her and putting his hand on her shoulder, a small touch, which was enough to turn her knees to jelly. Damn it.

"Nothing. Just girly stuff." She stood to move away from him as quickly as she could. "Where's your table?"

"All the way on the other side of the ballroom. Not as lucky this time as I was in San Francisco, sadly." He winked at Mary Lynn. "Did you tell her we'll both be part of your entourage in three months?"

"I did. She said you had great taste in agents."

He grinned. "Sounds like something *you'd* say, Mary Lynn."

"Okay, it was me. But I think she'd agree, wouldn't you, Cl ... ah ... April?"

Before Claudia could answer, the coordinator for the signing signaled "time" and the doors were opened. Brad leaned in, touched her face, and said softly, "After the reception tonight, can we have a repeat of last night?"

"You better get back to your table, hadn't you?" Claudia said.

"You haven't ..." Brad was interrupted by one of the volunteers who very firmly herded him across the room, leaving his sentence unfinished and his question unanswered.

Claudia relaxed into the buzz of all the readers and fans in the room talking to and buying books from their favorite romance authors. Some of the proceeds from the event went to a literacy program the organization supported, giving avid readers a great excuse to stock up on new books while feeling good about it because they were giving to a worthwhile cause.

Things were proceeding quite well until two women came to Claudia's table. As they thumbed through her books and loaded up on pens and key chains, one of them, glancing at her name tag, said, "Oh, you're from Seattle. I don't recall your name on the membership roster of the Greater Seattle Romance Writers of America. And I'm sure I've never seen you at the Emerald City Writers' Conference."

"No," Claudia answered. "I'm not a member. And I've never been to the conference."

"Well, we'll take care of that. I'm organizing the event next year, and I'd love for you to do a presentation. I had no idea someone so famous and so talented was living in our city!" She rummaged around in her bag until she found a scrap of paper, then picked up one of the pens from Claudia's display. "I need an e-mail or the name of your Facebook page so I can contact you." She held the pen in readiness to take down the information.

This was exactly what Claudia had been trying to avoid by refusing to attend these meetings. She could barely think straight; she was close to a full-blown panic attack. Luckily, Mary Lynn wasn't. She pulled a business card from her pocket. "I'm Mary Lynn Elliot, April's agent. How about you contact her through me, and I'll see what I can do for you?"

"Oh, that would be great," the woman said. "I can hardly wait to tell the other GSRWA members about this. They'll all want to come over to meet you."

She was as good as her word. At first, a small dribble of Seattleites came to Claudia's table. Then the dribble became a stream, which became a flood. It seemed every member of GSRWA in attendance went to see Claudia, bought her books, got her to sign them, and tried to wrest from her a promise to speak at next year's Emerald City Writers' Conference.

It was exhausting.

The minute the signing was over, Claudia bolted, leaving her agent to clean up after her. Her only thought was to escape, run home, get out of town. She was packing her suitcase when Mary Lynn returned.

"I thought I might find you doing that." She snatched the bag of makeup Claudia was about to pack and returned it to the bathroom. "Now listen to me, girlfriend. You are fine. There's no reason to panic. None of those women even came close to getting past your disguise. And I can handle whatever requests come from them. When they try to get you to speak at their conference or join their group, you'll be out of town, having life-saving surgery, meeting with the president— something. Don't worry. I'll take care of it."

"You don't understand. I can't do this anymore. All the lies. To Brad. To all these readers who tell me how much they love my work. Everyone trusts me, thinks they know who I am, and what do I do? Lie about it. They don't have a clue who I am. I'm beginning to think I don't have a clue who I am. I want to go back to being Claudia Manchester. If I can figure out who the hell she is anymore."

"Well, not to go all legal on you, but you just signed a contract for four more books as April Mayes. You have to continue to be her for a while. And not everyone is in the dark about who you are. I know. Your publisher knows."

"Yes, but you two have a vested interest in keeping me going as April."

"I have an interest in keeping a friendship going that means something to me, Claudia." She put an extra emphasis on the name. "I'm not using you as an ATM."

Claudia sank into the upholstered chair. "You're right. I'm sorry. I guess I'm a little upset."

"You are a master of understatement." Mary Lynn sat down next to her. "Look, why don't we put in an appearance at the reception long enough to keep the organizers happy and then get out of here for dinner someplace quiet so we can figure all this out."

"I don't know. I'm beginning to think the only way out of this is to move to another part of the country and start all over."

Mary Lynn hugged her. "Don't do that. I'd miss you. None of my other authors are nearly as interesting as you are."

Claudia sighed. "All right. I'll stay. For the moment. But if one more thing goes wrong, I'm gone."

"You've panicked about Brad. You've panicked about the Seattle romance writers' conference. What more could happen?" She stood and held out her hand to Claudia. "Come on. Let's get you dressed in some of your trashiest clothes and go have a glass of wine or two."

• • •

An hour later, Claudia was back in her room, madly throwing clothes, shoes, and toiletries into her suitcase. Mary Lynn had been wrong. So wrong. On a scale of one to ten wrong, she'd been a twenty. And now Claudia really had to get out of town.

The reception had started out okay. Brad was nowhere in sight and neither were the Emerald City women, which took some of the stress off her. Claudia had a glass of wine and a few hors d'oeuvres, chatted with several of the RWA staffers, and was finally beginning to relax when three women approached her and introduced themselves as members of the Rose City Romance Writers. They'd heard she lived in Portland, and they wanted to extend an invitation to join their chapter. She tried to brush them off by saying she lived in Seattle, but one of the women was most insistent she'd been told April Mayes was a Portlander.

Then, the final blow. The woman from the RWA chapter pointed out the person who was the source of the information about where Claudia lived. It was a faculty member from Portland State who taught women's studies and was working on a book about the role of romance novels in women's lives. Claudia didn't know how the woman recognized her, dressed as April Mayes, but apparently she did.

The jig was now well and truly up.

As soon as she was able to get away from the Portlanders and without saying good-bye to anyone or letting Mary Lynn know she was leaving, Claudia bolted from the reception and went to her room. She called the airline and changed her ticket to a flight leaving for Portland in three hours, then began to pack.

When that chore was finished, she wrote two notes. The first was easy.

Mary Lynn-

Everything is unraveling too fast for me to keep up with. I have to get out of here. Tell the conference organizers I got sick and apologize for my absence. I'll explain it all to you after you get home. Would you see that Brad gets the note in the envelope addressed to him? Thanks.

Claudia

The second note was more difficult to write. After three tries, what she came up with was:

Brad-

I can't do this anymore. You deserve better than the person I've been pretending to be. I'm going home to try to get my integrity back and my head straight. Please don't try to contact me. We'll both be better off if you don't.

April/Claire

She sealed the envelope, put it and the note to Mary Lynn on her friend's bed, and left the room. She fought back tears all the way to the airport and on the flight to Portland. It wasn't until she was safe in her own home that she let go and cried. And cried. And cried. Until she was sick of crying and went to bed.

Tomorrow, as Scarlett famously said, would be another day. And it had to be better than the one she'd just been through. Didn't it?

Chapter 15

Brad got to the reception late, thanks to a long phone call with his agent discussing the upcoming transition to Mary Lynn's agency. The event was in full swing when he got there, and the room was packed. He picked up a glass of wine and started looking for Claire. Twenty minutes later, waylaid by a dozen or more people but still Claire-less, he tracked down Mary Lynn. Together, they did what was close to a grid search of the room and, finding no Claire/April, went up to the room the two women shared. The first things he saw were the lone suitcase and the note on one of the beds.

Mary Lynn read it then handed him an envelope. "Cl ... April's left for home. She left this note for you."

"Left? Why? Did something happen in Seattle? Is she all right? Let me see your note." He tried to grab it but Mary Lynn tucked it in her jacket pocket.

"Personal. Sorry. Read yours."

He shook his head as he read it. "I don't understand. What can't she do anymore? And what does she mean, the person she's been pretending to be? I've always known about her pen name. I don't care about that. What the hell is going on? Explain it to me."

Mary Lynn wouldn't meet his gaze. And it seemed to take her a long time to find an answer. Finally she said, "It's not my place to explain anything about this. It's April's. You're going to have to track her down and ask her yourself."

He glared at her for a long moment, but she didn't look like she was about to give in to his fiercest stare. "God damn it, if you won't tell me what the hell is going on, that's exactly what I'm going to do." He grabbed the room phone and, in two calls, sent his regrets to the conference organizers for backing out of his panel the next day and changed his plane ticket.

From Portland to Seattle.

He saw Mary Lynn chewing a fingernail, but she kept quiet.

• • •

No one answered the door when Brad got to Claire's house in Seattle after flying from Denver. There was a damp package sitting on the porch that looked like it had been sitting in the summer rain for a couple days. No one had been there for a while, it seemed, which would track with her being in Denver. The name on the package wasn't Claire's. It was Mary Lynn's. He wondered why Mary Lynn had packages sent to her rental house when she knew Claire would be out of town, but where she got her online purchases delivered was the least of his concerns at the moment.

He flew home to Portland and began a campaign of e-mails, phone calls, and texts to Claire. There was never any response. He called Mary Lynn almost daily to see if she'd heard from her client and friend. She had not, and because of the worried tone in her voice, which was beginning to show, he believed her.

After a few days of being unable to get through to Claire using her personal contacts, he went for the big gun. He'd hunt her down at work. That's when the bombshell exploded. Bellevue College informed him there was not now nor had there ever been a Claire Mason employed in any capacity, certainly not as faculty. He checked out three different departments before he believed what they were telling him.

Claire had lied to him about where she worked? Why? Was she not really a teacher? He couldn't believe she was anything other than an educator. She was too confident in front of a group, imparted information too professionally. And her stories about her students and classes rang too true to have been made up. Not to mention her books showed extensive knowledge of English literature.

Maybe she was a high school teacher and thought it would sound more impressive if she said she was a college professor. In the hope he'd found the answer, he called every high school, public and private, in the Seattle area. It took him two weeks of free time to work his way through the list only to get nowhere.

Then, for good measure, he called every community college and university in the area. He came up dry there, too.

Once again, he tried to pry information out of Mary Lynn, confronting her with what he'd learned from Bellevue College. While she acknowledged she knew April didn't work there, she steadfastly refused to tell him anything else about April's private life. Saying she had been sworn to secrecy, she repeated what she'd said in Denver: He'd have to get the truth from the source. She claimed to have tried to get April to tell him herself while they were at dinner that first evening of the conference, but he wasn't sure he believed her. She also said she'd not heard from her client since they had returned from Colorado, and she was getting concerned. That he did believe.

He had reached the end of what he thought he could do to locate her. Somehow, this glorious woman had waltzed into and then out of his life, and he had no way of finding her again. The last thread of hope he had was trying to track her down at one of the big romance writers' conferences. The next one wasn't until after the first of the year. And since it was early fall, it meant it would be months before he had a chance to run into her again. Assuming she would even show up at the conference.

He tried to lose himself in work, which was more difficult than he expected, even though the start of a new school year was always a busy and exciting time. Every day that passed without coming up with some other way to find her frustrated him. He became withdrawn and moody with his colleagues, even had a difficult time being upbeat for his students. One of his best friends suggested he needed a vacation to clear his head. But winter break was a long way off.

He began to walk every day during his lunch hour, to think. Only a few blocks away from St. Mary's Academy, paralleling the main buildings of Portland State University, were the South Park Blocks, one of the jewels of downtown Portland. The twelve-block urban green space was full of towering old trees and pieces of public art and was bordered by many of the cultural institutions of the city. It was a pleasant, even restful, place to stroll and think. Or picnic, smoke dope, make out, pass out leaflets about every cause known to the student population. The activities were many and varied.

When he first started his daily walks there, Brad didn't pay much attention to what other people were doing. He used his walks as a time to be alone, to try to figure out what his next move should be. But as the days went by, and he couldn't come up with anything to do other than wait, he began to notice the young couples studying together, laughing, holding hands. They made him ache with missing Claire. Almost made him give up his walks, it hurt so much to think about what he didn't have anymore.

He also ignored, with more success, the hawkers trying to get passersby to take their fliers. Most of the time, Brad walked past them without even acknowledging them. But one afternoon, distracted by a woman with chestnut-colored hair, like Claire's, he absent-mindedly took a flier a student thrust in his hand as he walked past Lincoln Hall. He was about to dump it in a trashcan when what it said registered. There was a one-day seminar on teaching fiction in the twenty-first century going on in Lincoln Hall.

It sounded intriguing. The subject interested him. He had no more classes that day. He didn't want to go back to his office and face the sympathetic looks on the faces of his colleagues who had taken to dropping by his office, presumably to see if he was still among the living. Listening to some experts on a topic he found interesting, or at least diverting, might cheer him up. And to top it off, it was chillier than he had expected and being inside among strangers who wouldn't ask him questions wasn't the worst idea he'd had all day.

What the hell. The seminar was almost over, but he could still catch the last speaker. What did he have to lose? He went into the auditorium to listen.

The lights over the audience had been shut off and the lights on the stage were dim as the speaker behind the podium went through a PowerPoint presentation. The subject appeared to be a comparison of literary and commercial fiction. He couldn't see who was speaking, although he could tell from the voice it was a woman. A woman who sounded like someone he knew, although the mic was lousy and she kept getting feedback, which distorted her voice.

And what she was saying—he'd heard it before, hadn't he? It puzzled him. He couldn't put his finger on why it all seemed so familiar. He regretted not picking up the program with the list of presenters from the stack outside the auditorium. Maybe if he listened long enough, he'd figure out who it was and why she sounded familiar. Someone was bound to say her name during the question and answer session.

Then a slide flashed on the screen with a series of bullet points. As the woman began to expand on the first one, Brad scanned the list.

> *-Writers of genre fiction are assumed to be hacks or writers who can't make it in the world of literary fiction.*
>
> *-Good writing is good writing. Don't dismiss a book because it's shelved as "romance," "mystery," or "science fiction" or embrace bad writing because it's labeled "literary fiction."*

-Authors of commercial fiction want to give readers an escape, a heroine to admire, a hero to sigh over, a story that makes them think.

-Romance writers want to give readers a happily-ever-after; mystery writers want to reassure their readers good wins out over evil; sci-fi authors want their readers to know the aliens can't defeat the earthlings.

-If it's well written, it deserves the same respect the author of a mid-list literary fiction book gets.

It didn't take reading more than two of the bullet points before the light bulb in his brain went on. Of course he recognized the information. And, therefore, the speaker. But how …?

He ducked back into the hall and grabbed a program. The speaker was Claudia Manchester, PhD, Portland State University professor of English literature.

A.k.a. April Mayes. A.k.a. Claire Mason.

Jesus, if he was correct, he'd been searching all over Seattle for her and she'd been in his backyard the whole time. What the hell was this all about?

When the lights came back up, he confirmed what he already knew—the woman speaking was Claire. Claudia. Whoever. She was in a tailored suit, unlike anything he'd ever seen her wear, seemed to be wearing little or no makeup, and had her hair piled up on her head in a stylishly messy bun. She wasn't the hot April Mayes from San Francisco and Denver, and she wasn't the casual jeans-and-sweater Claire Mason from all those weekends they'd spent together.

His first thought was she must have one hell of a wardrobe to outfit all of her personas.

His irrelevant thought was rapidly followed by a mix of emotions he wasn't sure how to handle. As he watched her field questions from the audience, he was relieved his search was over. But not too far under the relief was anger at how she'd lied to him, as was a deeply embarrassed sense of having been had. Lastly, he was intellectually curious in an oddly detached sort of way about what the hell she thought she was up to and why she'd acted as she had.

The anger propelled him down the steps from the balcony and out into the Park Blocks to where the air was cool and he could breathe better, the auditorium having become unbearably stuffy. The head of steam he was building up almost exploded as he stood, shaking with anger, in the middle of the block, trying to decide what to do.

Should he go back to St. Mary's until he could come up with a plan? Hell, no. If his colleagues felt sorry for the sad and mopey Brad Davis, the played-for-a-fool Brad Davis would get even more pity and he was not in the mood for it. Neither was he confident he could hide how angry he was about what he had discovered.

Maybe he'd call Mary Lynn. Obviously she had known this little fact of Claire ... uh ... Claudia's life all along. They were friends, not merely agent and author. She had admitted as much when she said she had tried to convince Claire ...damn it ... Claudia to tell him the truth. They must have had a good laugh at his expense when the two of them gossiped about him. No, wait, they wouldn't have done that. If he knew anything, he knew they weren't cruel. Even so, why had Mary Lynn kept the information from him?

Ranting to Mary Lynn wouldn't get him what he really wanted, of course, which was an explanation and an apology from the source of his pain: Claire/Claudia/April. Maybe he should go to her office and wait for her, to see what her reaction would be. Maybe the element of surprise would get him what he deserved.

He knew the English Department offices were located in Neuberger Hall, and he wasn't very far away from the building. Why not? There was no sense wasting all this righteous indignation. He'd hunt her down, like he had in San Francisco. Only this time, he wasn't amused by Bambi's wily ways. He was mad. If she was lucky, his intellectual curiosity would kick in and he'd be able to control his temper long enough to demand what he wanted from her without yelling.

But intellectual curiosity never got a chance. Before he could take more than a few steps toward Neuberger Hall, Claire ... Claudia ... Bambi ... and a gaggle of other people, colleagues from the way they seemed to be talking to each other, crossed in front of him. They'd apparently gone out the side door of Lincoln Hall and come back to the Park Blocks to do the same thing he was doing—head for the English Department's offices. He stopped before his quarry could see him, then, after the group had gotten twenty yards ahead of him, followed, trying to decide exactly how to handle the situation.

He wasn't sure what triggered his next reaction. It could have been the carefree laughing he heard from the group she was in. Maybe it was because he thought surely she would sense his presence and turn to look but didn't.

Probably it was his temper getting the better of him. Whatever it was, he ran to close the distance between them, shouting her name as loudly as he could. The name, that is, she had given him. When she didn't respond to "Claire!" he changed tactics. Coming up behind her, he put his hand on her shoulder to stop her and said, "Aren't you April Mayes, the steamy romance writer?"

When she turned and registered who was talking to her, she got so pale he thought she was about to faint. He was almost ashamed to admit how much satisfaction he got from her reaction. Almost but not quite.

<h1 style="text-align:center">Chapter 16</h1>

It was a scene from Claudia's worst nightmare. She'd been feeling good about her presentation on commercial fiction. It had been well received. Even the two curmudgeons who didn't like "that sort" of writing said she'd done a good job presenting her case, although they hadn't changed their minds about the value of genre fiction in an academic setting. She'd gotten lots of applause, and her presentation had inspired good questions. Even as she'd worked her way out of the building, she'd gotten congratulations from colleagues who had already heard from other faculty members how thought provoking her talk had been.

In short, she felt like a success, something she hadn't felt like since, well, since before Denver. On top of everything else, it was a crisp fall day and she was walking through the Park Blocks laughing with colleagues who had no idea what hell she'd been going through for weeks. She felt free and happy and unburdened. Her colleagues were impressed with her work. The women's studies professor who had ratted her out in Denver hadn't surfaced since she got back. And she was unstuck writing her book. It was all going so very well.

Until someone called her by her pen name and she turned around to see Brad. The recent lack of attempts to communicate with her had led her to believe he had finally given up trying to contact her, which had been both a relief and a disappointment. She wanted to believe he'd walk through fire for her, and at the same time, she wanted him to go away so she wouldn't have to face him again.

Now, the worst had happened. Somehow he had tracked her down. She was facing him, all right. Here. On her home grounds. In front of the world—or at least, her world.

His sudden appearance made the blood leave her head and the muscle strength leave her knees. She took two steps back, feeling as if she were staggering, and tried to form a response that would get him away from her colleagues before he did any more damage. She hadn't yet found the words to respond to him when the chair of the English Department, Ann McNulty, came to her rescue. "Brad, what's wrong with you? This is Professor Manchester, not April Mayes." She pulled at Claudia's arm to get her to continue their walk.

Brad's smile barely moved his mouth and certainly didn't reach his eyes. "No, Professor McNulty, I'm afraid you're the one who's mistaken. This is April Mayes. Or maybe you know her as Claire Mason, the name she gave me."

"Claudia," Ann said, "do you know Brad Davis?" She was clearly confused, as were the five men standing around watching the interchange.

"Uh, yeah, I do. He teaches history at St. Mary's. Oh, you know that, don't you? I forgot, he teaches here sometimes, too."

Brad ignored her babbling. "You want to tell me what the hell's going on, Claire ... Claudia ... April ... whatever the hell you're calling yourself these days? I understand why you wanted to keep your romance writing secret and wrote under a pen name, but what I don't understand is why you gave me a fake name and lied about living in Seattle." He took a step closer to her.

"Although I guess this masquerade explains the New Seasons bags and how you knew so much about Abigail Scott Duniway."

New Seasons bags? What the hell is he talking about? Is he drunk?

Ann McNulty wasn't very big. She barely broke five feet and a hundred pounds. But she was a pit bull when it came to protecting her friends and colleagues. She stepped between Brad and Claudia and shook a finger at him. "Brad, I don't know what you want with Claudia, but I'd prefer you resolve whatever issue you have with her privately, not out in the middle of the Park Blocks and in front of all these people." She indicated the small groups of students drawn to the clutch of teachers by the raised voices. "If you can't get yourself under control, I'll call campus security." She waved a cell phone in front of him so he could see she was able to carry out her threat.

It didn't dissuade him one bit.

"I'd love to 'resolve our issues,'" he said. "But ever since we were together in Denver at the romance writers' convention this woman ..." He was tired of throwing all her names in her face. "This woman has refused to answer any of my texts or e-mails."

"Romance writers' convention?" one of the curmudgeons said. "I thought you were in Colorado visiting family. What were you doing at a romance writers' conference? Surely you don't ..." He stopped. Claudia could almost see the wheels turning in his head as he processed what Brad had said when he first accosted her. "My God. You write that trash?"

"It's not trash. She's a talented writer. Don't make judgments about her work until you read it," Brad said. But Claudia could see from the curmudgeon's expression the damage had been done. "Claire ... Claudia, talk to me."

"Talk to you? Why? You're filling the air with enough words right now for all of us. Enough words to ... I don't know ... sink my career, for example."

"Tell me why you lied to me. I deserve an explanation."

If Claudia had hoped he would give up or her colleagues would whisk her away from this horrible scene, her hopes were being hammered into the ground with every sentence Brad spoke. She was now not so much horrified as she was angry. "You deserve a slap in the face for what you're doing. Don't you understand? This," she swept her arm out to take in the whole scene, "this is exactly why I couldn't tell you the truth. I was afraid you'd do something, say something to out me. And, boy, was I right. Thanks to your little temper tantrum, a number of colleagues in my department and a healthy percentage of the student population of the university now know I write romance novels. You have made me the object of gossip and embarrassed me in front of faculty and strangers alike. If it was what you were aiming for, congratulations, you succeeded. You should be proud of yourself."

Tears began to form, but she didn't want to give him the satisfaction of seeing her cry over him. She had to end this confrontation before she broke down. "Go away, Brad. You've made your point. You found out who I am and where I work. Good for you. And you outed me to my colleagues just like you wanted to do. Hurray. Your job here is done. Now leave me alone."

She strode off, her colleagues forming a flying wedge around her. She hoped he wouldn't follow her to her office. Not only did she not want to talk to him but she knew the colleagues who were now protecting her would be full of questions when they were safely in the office. She had a lot of explaining to do.

•••

How the hell had his confrontation with Claire ... Claudia ... gone so wrong so fast? He had every right to be angry about the lies she'd told him. He had thought they were developing a loving, trusting relationship, but it turned out it was all phony. At least, on her part, if not on his. He'd bared his soul to her. Told her the secret he most feared being exposed, shared things about his family he'd never told anyone else. What he got in return, apparently, was nothing but a fabrication. Wasn't he entitled to an explanation of why she'd done it? Of course he was. But somehow, over the last few minutes, he'd been changed from wronged lover to the villain in the piece. How had it happened?

He wasn't sure he'd ever understand. So he turned to the more important question: What did he intend to do now that he knew how to find Claire ... damn it, *Claudia*? His first impulse was to follow her to her office, but it didn't take much reflection to reject the idea. The entire English Department was probably on alert for him if they weren't cross-examining Professor Manchester about her extra-curricular activities. He supposed he could wait until she left her office for home, but he didn't know where she parked her car, if she drove to work, where she'd exit the building, or when she usually left. He could be sitting outside on a chilly fall day for hours.

There was nothing to do but go back to his office.

On his way there, it occurred to him that, since Mary Lynn probably knew everything about the masquerade Claudia had tried to pull off, he could vent some of his righteous indignation at her. He called her as he walked along the street.

The call went immediately to voice mail, usually an indication she was on the phone with someone else. He left a message for her to call him and went back to his office where the papers from the first quiz of the year awaited grading. Luckily, it was a multiple-choice test and all he had to do was follow the key with the correct answers. If he'd had essays to grade, he'd have been sunk.

• • •

Mary Lynn hadn't called back by the time he left school, so when he got home, Brad poured himself a stiff drink and called her. She answered right away.

"Brad. Sorry I didn't return your call. I've had my hands full with another of my authors who's had an extremely bad day. Oh, wait. You already know about my other author since you're the cause of her problems."

"Her problems? How the hell did this become her problem? She lies to me, gives me a fake name, a fake address, hell, a fake *life* she's invented, and when I try to get an explanation, I'm the bad guy? I feel like a fool for falling for her ... falling for her story, that is. And don't try to get yourself off the hook. You must have known what was going on all along." By the time he was finished with his rant, he was pacing the floor.

The silence at the other end of the call stopped him in his tracks. She was going to try to evade his question, he was sure.

"Don't you lie to me, too. You knew, didn't you?" he prodded.

"Yes, you're right. I knew." Mary Lynn sighed. "I even helped her create Claire Mason. I got her a cheap phone in her name and loaned her my house for you two to have a place in Seattle to meet."

"At least she told me one truth. She said the house was yours and I assumed she meant she rented from you. It also explains why the house didn't look like I expected her place to look."

"I don't want to hear complaints about my taste in decorating, thank you very much. I love cabbage rose slipcovers."

"Your taste in slipcovers isn't what I want to talk about. Why, Mary Lynn? Why did you two do this? What did I ever do to either one of you to deserve this kind of treatment?" By this time, he was almost yelling into the phone, he was so frustrated.

"If you'll dial back the temper and the tone of your voice, I'll try to explain."

He took a deep breath and dropped into his favorite leather chair. "I'm listening," he said in as controlled a tone as he could manage.

Mary Lynn explained in detail how she and Claudia had created an identity for her to keep him from connecting her with Portland in any way so there was no risk of her colleagues finding out about her secret life as a romance writer. She ended the long story by saying, "And now, all the effort she's put into working for tenure would seem to be down the drain because of what you revealed to half the tenure committee this afternoon. Including the two members of the committee who hate commercial fiction and don't believe a tenured professor should be writing it."

"It's not a good explanation, but at least it's some explanation." Brad wasn't about to give up his status as the aggrieved victim easily.

"Claudia has been working for tenure forever. It's her holy grail, the sign she's made it, that she's secure in her job. And now she's sure—with good reason, I might add—it's slipped out of her reach. Maybe for good."

He groaned. "Shit. I didn't mean to mess things up. When I found out her real name by accident, my first reaction was she'd played me for a fool with her lies. I couldn't think of any reason for what she did. All I wanted was an explanation."

"How *did* you find out who she is? She was crying so hard I didn't have the heart to ask too many questions."

"I imagine she thinks I ran across her walking in the Park Blocks, but what really happened was I chanced on a lecture she was giving and recognized her." A lump in his throat was making it difficult to speak. "She was crying?"

"In all four phone calls this afternoon and this evening. I've never seen or heard her cry before. It sounded pretty messy."

"Jesus. All I wanted was the truth. The last thing I wanted was to make her cry. I have to do something to make this right. Can you think of anything I can do?"

"Yes. Nothing. She has to work this out herself."

"Then you think she can still find a way to convince the tenure committee ...?"

"I doubt it. I talked to the head of the English Department myself an hour ago. She was very apologetic but said tenure was no longer likely for Claudia this year. I tried telling her how successful Claudia was and how well respected she was in the business, but I couldn't make her reconsider. It's all over for now. Maybe for the foreseeable future."

"If you can't do anything, I have to. I love her. I can't sit back and let her life be ruined because of me. I have to do something."

Very softly, Mary Lynn said, "Don't you think you've done enough already?"

It didn't occur to him until much later that she never questioned his saying he loved Claudia.

Chapter 17

It took Brad a few days to figure out what he could do to help clean up the mess he'd made by confronting Claudia—he was beginning to get used to calling her by her real name, which surprised him at first until he remembered he'd never thought she was a Claire to begin with. When he came up with his plan, it took a few more days to put it into action. But less than a week after the disastrous scene in the Park Blocks, he was dodging raindrops and students doing the same on his way to Neuberger Hall where he had an appointment with the head of the English Department.

Ann McNulty left him sitting in the reception area almost twenty minutes past the time of their appointment before coming out of her office to greet him.

"I'm sorry to keep you waiting. I was on the phone with the president of the university, following up on the little scene we were both involved in a week ago."

Brad hoped he kept the guilty flinch he felt from showing. "I apologize for what happened. I really don't have an excuse for my behavior except to say I was caught off guard by ... well, by learning Professor Manchester was someone I knew under another name."

"Yes, she's explained it all to me. If you've come to apologize, you've done so and I accept it." She put her hand out to him as if to dismiss him with a handshake. "Now, I need to get back to ..."

"That's not why I'm here." He shook his head in frustration. "Well, it's part of why I'm here." He held up the carrier bag he was holding. "The other part of why I'm here is in this bag. Can we go into your office so I can show you?"

The look of concern—fear, even—on her face brought him up short. Did she really think he was holding something dangerous? Did he look like a carrier bag bomber? "It's nothing harmful.

Only books," he said, opening the bag and tilting it so she could see inside. "I'd like to talk to you about them in private."

She stared at him for longer than he was comfortable with before saying, "All right. I have ten minutes until my next appointment," and led him into her office.

He closed the door. The nervous look on the professor's face hadn't relaxed, and she was now playing with a letter opener in a manner that made him think of how it could be used as a weapon. He had to bring down the anxiety level in the office quickly. Slowly, keeping eye contact with her the whole time, he took four books out of the bag and began to lay them on her desk, one at a time.

"This one is based on *Pride and Prejudice*." He put the second book on top of the first. "This one retells *The Tempest*." The third and fourth ones joined their companions. "This one uses the story of *A Christmas Carol* and this one *Sense and Sensibility*." He reached in the bag for two more books. "Here we have a story based on *Twelfth Night*. Last but not least, and one of my favorites, a retelling of *The Importance of Being Earnest*."

"And your point is?"

"My point is I want you to look at the author's name." When she looked up rather sharply at him, he added, "Please."

Professor McNulty picked up one book after another and skimmed the back cover copy. He saw the exact moment when the penny dropped.

"These are all Claudia—Professor Manchester's—books."

"Exactly. There are a couple more, but these are the ones I've read so far. She's working on a rewrite of *Romeo and Juliet*, by the way. It gives the kids a chance to have a life together in the end."

"Why did you bring these to me?"

"I created the problem she's having, and I want to try to straighten it out. I'm guessing she hasn't said much about what she writes other than to say it's romance so I thought I'd be the one to give you the pleasure." He sat in the chair opposite the professor's desk. "You know I write historical romances in addition to teaching at St. Mary's. I've never had a problem with my writing life interfering with my teaching life, and I don't understand why it should be a problem for her."

Ann snorted. "Your work is a bit different, don't you think? I've read several of them. They'd not the kind of steamy romances Claudia says she's written." She was flipping through one of the books as she spoke. Perhaps he had caught her attention after all.

"True. But I knew when I started that I had to be more careful. My student population is a lot younger than Claudia ... ah, Professor Manchester's ... is." He leaned on the desk. "She doesn't deserve to have her work for the university dismissed because of where her beautifully written books are shelved in Barnes and Noble. And she shouldn't be punished because she was reluctant to tell you about her extracurricular activities when she knew there were people in the department who would disdain her work without even reading it."

"I think you're being a little unfair. We all appreciate the work Professor Manchester does for our students. She's one of our most popular teachers. Every year, a number of students change majors and end up becoming teachers themselves because of her passion for literature and for her students."

"Then why are you denying her tenure?"

"What makes you think she's being denied tenure?"

"A conversation with her agent. Who, it happens, is about to become my agent. So we're close." With luck, Mary Lynn, if asked, would let his white lie about their "closeness" slip by.

"Oh, I see." Professor McNulty squirmed in her chair. "Well, yes, the tenure committee has tentatively voted to put off offering Claudia tenure. Not a denial exactly but ..."

"But it works out the same—no tenure."

"I suppose you're right, although there hasn't been a final vote yet. Besides, what exactly do you think I can do about it? I'm only one member of the committee."

"One member with a great deal of influence, I'll bet, if academic politics are the same here as they are everyplace else I'm familiar with."

He was rewarded with a small smile and a slight shrug of one shoulder.

"What I want you to do is be fair. Before you make a final decision, read one or two of Professor Manchester's books. See how good she is. Get other members of the committee, the ones who might have open minds, to do the same. Surely you understand the attention she can bring with her success as a writer. That must be important to the head of the department."

"I'm not sure we want the kind of attention steamy romances would give us."

"Just read the books. The love scenes are as well written as every other part of the book, and her readers love her for them. There's not one crude or vulgar word in all those books combined. Hell, even I use a crude word or two in my books, and no one thinks it makes them trash."

"No, I did some research on you before I asked you to guest lecture the first time. As I said, I've read some of your books. Your impeccable research is what impressed me. Before all this happened, I was even thinking there might be a place for your books in one of our summer classes for nondegree students."

"Thanks, but I'm more interested in having you read Claudia's books right now."

Brad watched Ann chew on her lip for a moment, her gaze flitting from one book cover featuring a headless, shirtless man to another with the same type of image. "I do wish the covers weren't so ...so ..."

"Tawdry? Yeah, it's a convention in the romance world that a number of people dislike, including Claudia. She's trying to get some say in selecting a cover, which might make a difference down the line, but it's a hard sell."

Ann rose and put out her hand. This time, Brad took it. She said, "All right. I'll read one of these and pass a couple along to other members of the tenure committee. That's all I can promise you."

"That's all I'm asking. Claudia's talent will do the rest. I guarantee it."

Chapter 18

Claudia had been dragging her tail feathers for almost ten days. She had finally stopped crying about the situation, accepting the blame for her role in what she was calling "The Debacle in the Park." After all, she was the one who'd wanted to keep her secret life as a romance writer hidden. She was the one who invented the backstory of another life for Brad. She was the one who fell hard for him but couldn't find a way to tell him the truth.

But he was the one who brought it all crashing down around her ears. If she didn't love him so much, she'd hate him.

Her classes were going well, which was a blessing. Her writing certainly wasn't. She hadn't even looked at her new book since their confrontation. Trying to plot a positive outcome for Ross and Jules, her Romeo and Juliet stand-ins, was a little difficult when she couldn't find a positive outcome for her own life.

Mary Lynn checked in with her on a regular basis, to make sure she hadn't done anything stupid, like run away again. Her friend knew her well enough to know she'd never do anything to harm herself, but her track record did include bolting. Especially recently.

But nothing lightened the gray atmosphere surrounding her. She got through her days trying to be upbeat and interesting for her students while saving the gloom and doom for when she was home. Alone. It worked pretty well. She found comfort in her routine, enjoyment from watching students fall in love with literature, and solace at home reducing her To Be Read pile of books.

Then one Friday, a couple weeks after the Debacle in the Park, she got a message in her e-mail inbox asking her to come to Ann McNulty's office when she was finished with classes for the day.

It could only be one thing—the tenure committee had met and made a final decision. She had been turned down.

It was a long day for her. Even her most oblivious students noticed she was off. Several asked if she was feeling okay. One young man, who had been a royal pain in the butt over having to read a second Jane Austen novel, even volunteered to go get her coffee after class was over, a kind gesture that brought tears close to the surface.

But then, almost everything brought tears today.

Finally, her classes were finished. Claudia went to the ladies' room to comb her hair and refresh the little makeup she wore. A new coat of lipstick wouldn't make the news any easier to bear, but at least she could look good while she got it.

Ann was waiting with her office door open when Claudia arrived. "Come on in, Claudia. Close the door and have a seat. Can I get you a coffee or something?"

"Thanks but I'm coffee-ed out for the day. But if you want something ..."

"No, I was being hospitable, hoping you'd be more comfortable with a hot drink."

"Offering a last meal for the dead woman walking?"

Ann cocked her head and frowned. "That's an interesting— even creative—way of looking at this meeting. No wonder you have such a devoted fan base."

Claudia wasn't sure what she meant and was even less sure she wanted to ask for an explanation.

Ann went to the other side of her desk and sat. She picked up a book from a pile to her right and said, "Over the past week or so, I've read several good books by an author I was unfamiliar with. They were well-written, beautifully plotted, interesting updates of classic literature. Several other members of the department have read them, too."

Claudia still didn't know where this was going but thought it wise to appear interested in what seemed to be a random conversation about literature. "Written by anyone I would know?"

"Oh, yes. I'd say you know this author quite well. Her name is April Mayes."

Claudia was stunned. And silent. When she could finally speak, she said, "You read my books? Why?"

"A friend of yours brought six of them to me recently and insisted I read them. I was reluctant at first, but once I read the first one, I couldn't stop myself. I had to read more. I passed them along to three other colleagues. We all had the same reaction. You are a wonderful writer, and your clever use of classic literature is brilliant." She leaned back in her chair. "The only thing we can't figure out is why you'd want to hide your talent the way you have been."

Claudia swallowed hard, trying not to choke up. "You read my books? My romances? Really?"

"Yes, really. But you didn't answer my question. Why did you keep this hidden from us ... from me?"

"I was sure no one would accept the genre. It would stand in the way of my getting tenure. And I was right, wasn't I? Because of what happened after my lecture on commercial fiction, the tenure committee voted to deny me tenure."

"Not quite accurate—they voted to delay a decision—but I can see how you'd think what you do."

"The outcome is the same. They'll never give me tenure now."

"That's actually not true. We met earlier today, and the vote was six to two in your favor."

Claudia was stunned. Stunned, relieved, and sure if she didn't get herself under control, the few tears she could feel leaking from her eyes would be joined by hundreds of their relatives. The thing she had worked for all her career, which had seemed out of reach only a few minutes before, had just dropped into her lap with a far stronger vote of support than she had ever imagined she'd get.

Ann continued, "I don't imagine you have to ask who the two no votes were."

Laughter now bubbled through the tears, and Claudia almost choked before she got out, "No, I'm sure Statler and Waldorf voted against me."

"Who are Statler and Waldorf?" Ann handed her a tissue.

Claudia wiped her eyes and blew her nose before answering the question. "The two old guys on the *Muppet Show* who sat in the balcony and always had bad things to say about what was going on. Those curmudgeons on the committee remind me of cranky Muppets."

"And that will be an image I'll never be able to shake now, thank you very much. I shouldn't laugh, but it fits them perfectly." She stood and walked to the other side of her desk. "I normally give newly tenured professors a hearty handshake, but you deserve a hug." She acted on her words. "I have to tell you, however, there was one condition for your tenure."

"Do you want me to stop writing romances? I've signed a contract for four more, and I don't know if I can—"

"No, no. Quite the opposite. We want you to claim your place in the Portland literary world. First of all, we want you to 'come out' as a romance writer. Then we want to have you help us explore the possibility of a minor in commercial fiction for the English department. Other places are developing similar programs. Seton Hill even has an MFA in it."

"Oh, my God, Statler and Waldorf must have had apoplexy when you suggested that."

"We had already floated the idea of a curriculum change after the lecture you gave on the subject so they weren't exactly surprised. They weren't thrilled, either, but they will be massively outvoted. We'll be discussing it at the next departmental meeting so can I ask you to do a little research on the subject to bring before the group? Find out which schools are doing something similar and if there's any research on how successful the programs are."

"I'd be happy to. And I can't thank you enough for supporting me like this. It means the world to me." She started toward the door. "One more thing. You said a friend of mine brought you the books. I assume it was my agent, Mary Lynn Elliot?"

"Oh, she called all right. Several times. I enjoyed talking to her. I see why you're friends as well as professionally connected. But she wasn't the person who brought the books to me."

Not Mary Lynn? Who then? Who else would have done something like that? Could have done it? Her old fear of being exposed as a fraud made a brief appearance until her curiosity overpowered it. She had to know the answer. "Can you tell me who it was, then?"

"You mean you don't know?"

"No, I don't. No one other than Mary Lynn knows my real name. Well, except my publisher, but they're in New York."

"You're forgetting one other person, Claudia."

"Who?"

"Brad Davis."

Chapter 19

Brad half expected, maybe even half hoped, Claudia would contact him when she found out he'd gone to her department head. How she would react to what he'd done was another story. But as days passed and she didn't contact him, he gave up hoping. At least not hearing from her meant he wouldn't have to worry what she would say about his meddling, yet again, in her professional life.

Mary Lynn told him the tenure committee had voted in Claudia's favor. His new agent was positive his intervention had been what tipped the scales. He no longer had to carry around the guilt about screwing up Claudia's chance to get what she'd worked so hard for.

Nothing, however, could help him shake a certain melancholy. He'd hoped for so much from the relationship with Claudia. Maybe too much. Maybe that was the problem. He'd been seeing happily-ever-after. She'd been seeing happily-for-now. Which had become happily-for-then.

Or maybe it was just the fall days gradually getting shorter, dusk coming earlier, and the rainy season setting in for its long winter run. This time of year always had the effect of making him a bit sad and serious.

A friend wanted to set him up with a blind date who he said was hot, beautiful, and starry-eyed about the chance to date a real author. Brad gently refused. He hated blind dates. They always ended up making him wonder how the friend who was setting him up knew so little about him that he thought the woman he'd recommended would interest Brad. And he was seriously not up to a one-on-one with a starry-eyed fangirl.

The only thing making him happy was his writing. He got the manuscript for his new book finished months ahead of his deadline, the research that usually took him a year getting done in a few months of intense work instead. When he'd sent it to Mary Lynn to review, she'd raved. So had the history professor at Lewis & Clark College who was his reader for historical accuracy.

With one book finished and off to his publisher, he outlined the next one—a book on the Chinese Exclusion Acts. Hours spent in the Oregon Historical Society happily searching out reference materials and old photographs were hours during which he didn't have to think about Claudia Manchester, the relationship they'd had, or what had happened to it. He was beginning to think he should move into the building, it was such a comforting place to be, mostly because it held no memories of his failed romance.

Enough time eventually passed for him to feel pretty sure he was over Claudia. Then he went to a reading at the Mt. Tabor Presbyterian Church, which was not far from his home in Southeast Portland. The reading was in an elegant room dubbed Taborspace. With old wood and stained glass windows setting the mood, it was an ideal site for lectures and readings. He often wandered over without knowing who would be there, hoping it was something interesting. On this night, he hit on a poetry reading by Christopher Luna, the poet laureate of Clark County across the river in Washington State. After a delightful reading and a short chat with the man, Brad took a look at the list of upcoming events to see if there were any he couldn't miss.

His heart missed a beat when he saw listed for the following week, "A reading from *Ross and Jules*, a work in progress by Claudia Manchester, writing as April Mayes." It was sponsored by the Rose City Romance Writers and billed as the very first public reading by the author.

He debated for days whether to attend. One day, he'd think he wanted to see her. The next day, he didn't think he could bear it. Certainly, he was curious about how she'd react to seeing him. Would she smile at him? Hug him? Hit him? Hate him?

In the end, he decided he wanted to hear her voice again, see her big brown eyes, watch the light shine on her hair, red or not, with or without extensions. Even if it turned out to be the last time, he wanted to drink in how beautiful she was and hear her read from the book she'd been working on when they had their weekend at the Washington Coast, which now seemed like another life.

The place was packed when he got there, so crowded he had to join the standing room group in the back. He was happy for Claudia. This would certainly spike sales of her books, a table full of which was already arranged in the outer hall in anticipation of just such a result. He immediately spotted her at the front of the room, talking with several women. She wore a midcalf-length skirt and a sweater. Her hair was piled up in a soft bun. It was what he now knew was her Professor Manchester look. The only concession to her April Mayes persona was the pair of stilettos she was wearing and her bright red lipstick. She looked lovely, confident, and in charge. Not sure whether he wanted her to see him, he kept out of her line of sight and watched as she laughed with the women, leaning closer to hear them over the buzz in the room. Right at seven o'clock, one of the women asked for quiet and announced the reading was about to begin.

•••

Claudia was more nervous than she'd ever been in a decade of teaching at the university level. She hadn't expected this kind of turnout, although the Taborspace organizers had warned her it was likely to be full based on the dozens of calls they'd had asking for information about time and date.

Her mouth was dry so she gulped half her glass of water, then refilled it from the pitcher on the table beside the lectern. The original plan had been for her to sit and read from her manuscript, but with this many people in the room, they had to do something else. She'd have to use the lectern so everyone could see and hear her, which she hated doing because it felt like she had a barrier between her and the audience. But it couldn't be helped.

She listened as the president of the Rose City Romance Writers introduced her in such glowing terms, Claudia wasn't sure she could possibly live up to the hype. And she said so when she began to speak.

"I'm tempted to thank the Rose City Romance Writers and Taborspace for inviting me here this evening and ask if there are any questions before I sit down and shut up. I surely cannot live up to the description of the woman you heard introduced. She is not, I assure you, me. Thank you, Madame President, for making me sound so much more impressive than I really am."

When the laughter died down, she continued. "But since I make a living standing in front of any audience that'll sit still long enough to pay attention, I won't. Seeing this wonderful turnout brings out the lecturer in me, I'm afraid, and encourages me to do this more often."

Applause interrupted her. As she waited for it to finish, she scanned the room, looking for ... she wasn't sure what. Someone familiar maybe? She told herself no one she knew was likely to be there. Certainly, the face she would love to see was not going to be there. He hadn't contacted her in weeks. Not that she'd expected him to. She was the one who should have made contact to at least thank him for what he did to help her with the tenure committee. She had blamed her lack of manners on being too embarrassed, too humiliated by the scene in the Park Blocks that day. In truth, she was ashamed at the way she'd lied to him about who she was the whole while they were together and not sure how to even begin to apologize for that. Given how she'd treated him while they were together and the way in which they parted, why would she even imagine he'd show up to hear her read?

"Anyway, as you may know, I've been writing under a pen name for some time now. Only recently have I come out into the light, so to speak. In fact, this is the first time I've ever read my work in public. So I'd appreciate it if you'd be gentle with me tonight."

More laughter and a smattering of applause.

"If you've read any of my other books, you might have recognized some familiar plotlines. I confess I'm one of those writers who steals stories from other authors."

"Like Shakespeare," someone in the audience called out.

"Wow. Even the introduction didn't go so far as to compare me to Shakespeare. Thank you. However, I assure you in four hundred years, no one will be reading my work, but if the human race survives, they'll still be reading his."

She took another sip of water. "Part of the reason is the universality of his stories. They speak to us in every generation. And they provide the inspiration for other writers. He has provided me with several ideas for my books including the work in progress I'll be reading from tonight. I've also used Jane Austen, Charles Dickens, and Oscar Wilde as inspiration. Teaching English lit is a real advantage when it comes to trying to find plot devices, it turns out.

"So, enough talking about the work. How about I read from what I'm working on? This book, as I said, is loosely based on a Shakespeare play. I decided *Romeo and Juliet* needed a chance at a happily-ever-after so I'm rewriting them as 'Ross and Jules,' the son and daughter of two restaurateurs who hate each other. The fathers have spent their entire careers competing with each other, sabotaging one another's operations, and trying to pass along the enmity to their children. But the hero and heroine meet at a fund-raising event, a masquerade, and begin to date. She discovers who he is, and because she's afraid he won't love her if he knows who she really is, she hides her true identity from him while at the same time hiding his identity from her family." She bit the inside of her lip to keep herself from adding how experienced she was at that particular skill.

"Here's how I pictured their first meeting."

And she began to read the scene where Ross and Jules are introduced.

•••

It was clear now he was not over this woman. Might never be over her. Listening to her talk, watching her graceful gestures, Brad was once more reminded how she captivated him. She was everything he could ever want in a woman, and he had lost her because of one foolish outburst.

The plot of her book as she described it tonight was closer to the one she'd told him about in Denver than it was to what he'd heard her read while they were at the beach. He'd never made the connection before, but had she told him the story at dinner that night as some sort of warning about what she was doing? Should he have picked up on it and asked questions? No. Of course not. Why would he? He'd had no reason to think she was hiding her true identity from him. Although, he had thought she was keeping *something* from him. Had he been so dense as to not understand what she was trying to say?

Claudia had gotten to the end of her reading and was answering questions. He was making his way through the standing room crowd in the back, having decided to slip out the door before he gave in to the impulse to grab her and kiss her in front of all her newly acquired fans, when a woman asked, "How does Jules tell Ross the truth about who she is so they can have their happily-ever-after?"

This answer he wanted to hear.

<h1 style="text-align:center">Chapter 20</h1>

It was the question Claudia had most hoped to avoid. But she had to answer it. "The only thing that will work, I think, is for him to discover it himself in some way and confront her. It'll be the equivalent of the scene at the tomb in Shakespeare's play. But this time, they'll have another chance at love."

"Because our romances need happy endings," the questioner said.

"They certainly do," Claudia said. "Because the romances we have in real life don't always have them." As she said it, she scanned the crowd hoping to see nodding heads from the women attending. Maybe even from the sprinkling of men there.

Instead, what she saw, at the back of the room, was a face she still saw in her dreams. Brad was there.

But as soon as he realized she'd seen him, he started for the door. She had to see him. She couldn't let him go without saying something, several somethings, to him.

"Thank you so much for coming, everyone. I'm going to take a quick break, and then I'll be at the table signing books. Please have a cup of coffee or a cookie, and I'll be right back."

Without waiting to explain to the surprised hosts for the evening, she pushed her way through the crowd and ran out the door. When she got to the sidewalk, she looked up and down the street, afraid he had already driven away. Then she saw him in the next block, walking rapidly away from the church.

She tried running after him, but the stilettos she was wearing at Mary Lynn's suggestion wouldn't let her. She was beginning to get used to them, but running was still out of the question. And it was too damn cold to take them off and run barefoot. So she did the only thing she could. She yelled. Loudly. "Brad! Wait up, will you?"

He stopped and turned around. When she got closer to him, she could see he was wearing the Aran sweater she remembered from San Francisco and his leather jacket with the collar turned up against the chilly drizzle; his hands were jammed in the jacket pockets. "What can I do for you, Claudia?" He was using his teacher's voice, not the warm, sexy one she heard in her dreams.

"I ... uh ... I was surprised to see you. Thank you for being here."

"I come here often. Taborspace is only a couple blocks from my house, and I like to support fellow Portland writers." He seemed to emphasize the word *Portland.*

"It was my first public reading so it was nice to see a familiar face in the audience."

"I wanted to hear how your work in progress was doing. You read some of it to me at the beach, remember?"

Remember? How could she forget? She remembered every detail of every day they'd spent together. Not to mention every night. Especially every night.

"Well, I was happy to see you. I ... uh ... I have been meaning to call you for a while. Or e-mail you. Text. Something. I mean ... I should have been in touch to thank you for what you did." She felt awkward and stupid, stumbling with words as though English was her second language.

"What did I do to deserve your thanks?" His tone had changed a little. He sounded ... well, she wasn't sure what he sounded like, but he wasn't quite as detached and remote as he had first been. And he was baiting her, she was sure. He knew very well what he'd done.

"You went out on a limb to speak to Ann McNulty, of course, and asked her to read my books."

"Oh, that." His mouth twitched as if he were trying to suppress a smile.

"Yes, that. It made all the difference in the world."

"It was the least I could do since I was the one who screwed things up for you. It was my way of apologizing for what I did when I confronted you after your lecture. I heard from Mary Lynn the committee voted to give you tenure. Congratulations."

She hoped he would want to shake hands with her, hug her, something. She wanted to feel his touch more than she had ever wanted anything. But he kept his hands in his pockets. "Because of you, I not only got tenure but am heading up a committee to look into the possibility of adding a commercial fiction minor to our department."

"That's great. Congratulations again."

"We might be looking for guest lecturers on the subject. Would you be interested? There probably wouldn't be any money in it and the classes would be small at first, I'm sure, but it might give you a chance to reach a few new readers."

The smile finally broke through. "You need to work on your sales pitch a bit. But, yes, I guess I'd consider it. Why don't you tell Mary Lynn when the program gets going, and she can let me know?"

"Mary Lynn. Sure. I'll contact Mary Lynn."

An awkward silence seemed to drag on for hours, although Claudia was sure it was really only a few moments. Brad broke the silence. "I shouldn't keep you out here in the cold any longer."

"I'm okay. I wanted to thank you."

"And you have." He turned to walk away.

"Brad, wait. There's something else I have to say to you. I need to say I'm sorry."

His back still to her, he said, "Sorry for what?"

"Do you really have to ask? For lying to you. For not being honest about who I was. For all those things I said that weren't true."

"'All those things'? Meaning ...?"

"My name. Where I worked. The house in Seattle."

He finally turned and faced her. "Is that all you lied about?"

"Isn't it enough?"

"In one way, I suppose it is, but humor me. You owe me that, at least, don't you?"

She was sure he was playing on her guilt, but even if he was, she had to admit he was right. She did owe him. If he wanted a detailed list of every untruth she'd told him, she'd give it to him. "The only other lies were my Seattle phone number and the Claire e-mail address. They were real enough but still part of a lie. And you know—well, I guess you always knew—the way I dressed and how I looked as April Mayes wasn't real either."

"That wasn't particularly hard to figure out."

"The one thing I never lied about was how much I loved being with you. I know I messed it up beyond all recovery with my fake identity. But I didn't lie about my feelings or how much our relationship meant to me."

He let out a sigh, and his shoulders seemed to relax. "Thank you. I needed to know."

"And I tried to tell you the truth. Or at least, made a little foray into trying to. Sort of."

"Was it at dinner in Denver? When you were talking about your book?"

"Yes. I thought maybe you'd figure it out, and I wouldn't have to ... oh, I don't know what I thought. I was scared you'd be angry. And you were, when you did find out. Like I was afraid you'd be."

Another silence, this time broken by Claudia. "Well, that's all I wanted to say to you. So, I guess I should go." She had to get out of there before she broke down and blubbered. This man had set her on the edge of tears more times than the sum total of everyone else she'd ever met in her life. He apparently still had the power to get her there.

She hadn't gone more than half a block back toward the church when he called to her.

"Claudia? How sorry are you, exactly?"

She whirled around. "What do you mean?"

He started walking toward her. "I thought the question was pretty clear. But I can rephrase it. On a scale of one to ten, how sorry are you?"

"Twenty. Thirty, maybe. As sorry as I can be on any scale."

"Sorry enough to make you willing to try to pick up where we left off, before all the crazy stuff got in the way?"

His question stunned her. She hadn't heard from him in weeks. Had only her memories and some hot dreams to keep her company ever since the incident in the Park Blocks. His anger then had convinced her he would never, ever be able to get past what she'd done so they could be together. His lack of contact since then seemed to support her belief.

But here he was asking if she could pick up where they left off. He opened his mouth, as if he had more to say, but stopped, his eyes searching her face for something, some sign, maybe, of what she thought.

Could she give him what he was asking? She wasn't sure. How could a relationship based on lies ever succeed? Was it really possible to go on as if it hadn't happened?

"How could we? Why would you do that?"

"Why? Surely you know the answer." His voice now was soft, sweet as honey in her ears.

She was still afraid, still not sure. She shook her head and saw the expression on his face turn from hope to bleak acceptance. "No, I don't think I do. But in any case, picking up where we left off isn't a good idea. I mean, how do you go on when the whole beginning was a lie?"

He didn't answer.

"Say something, Brad. Anything. Please."

"Not sure what there is to say. You're pretty clear we can't try to pick up the pieces, so what's left?" He looked as if he were about to leave.

An idea began to take shape in her head. "Wait. I don't think we can reconstruct something true out of bits of real life and large chunks of fake identities. But maybe, instead of trying to glue it all back together, we could rewind."

"I don't understand." A smile was flickering around the corners of his mouth as he took a step toward her.

"If we go back to the start, begin again, maybe ..."

"How would we do that?" The whole smile was there again, the one she loved because it made her heart beat faster and her knees melt.

"Well, we could begin with what I should have done the first time I saw you."

"Which is?"

"I walk up to you and say, 'Hi, my name is Claudia Manchester. I'm an English literature professor who's dressed this way because I also write romance novels, and I'm on my way to a conference. If you're waiting for the plane to San Francisco, too, we have ninety minutes before we board. Can I buy you a drink?'"

Brad now sported a huge grin. The shoulders she loved were relaxed and coming closer as he took the remaining steps needed to be so close to her she was sure none of the drizzle was getting between them. "I think I'd have said, 'My name is Brad Davis. Thanks, but I'm not in the mood for a drink.' Then I'd take a chance and show you what I *was* in the mood for." He lowered his head and claimed her mouth in a kiss. When he broke from it, he said, "Is that what you mean by rewinding?"

"That's moving a bit faster than we would probably have moved in the middle of the airport, but I'm okay with it."

"Let me take another chance, then. I love you. I don't give a damn what your name is, where you live, how you dress, or what you write. I love you, and I want you back in my life. I'll rewind, pick up pieces, glue things together—whatever you want, to make it happen."

She collected her thoughts for a few seconds before responding, long enough for a worried look to appear on his face. "But you were going to leave the reading without saying anything to me."

He touched her cheek, his expression now tender and sweet. "I didn't want to make a public scene and embarrass you again."

"And you haven't tried to get in touch with me for ages."

"I can say the same for you."

"Well, if ..."

"No more ifs, ands, or buts, Professor. Just tell me if there's a chance."

"There's more than a chance. I love you, too."

He kissed her again. "That's a relief. Now let's go finish your book signing. Then I'll take you to my house. I want to make love to you and call you by your real name, assuming I can remember what it is when we're in bed together."

Claudia's laugh might have been heard a block away.

"It wasn't that funny, was it?" Brad asked.

"I just realized. You may be the only man on the planet who has gotten away with calling the woman he's making love with by another woman's name." She tucked her arm through his. "But please notice that's in the past tense. From now on, it better be the right one."

Jack Richardson knew what was coming as soon as Anne Salazar said, "We need to talk." He even felt a sense of relief that it was finally happening.

"I'm listening, Anne," he said.

She put on her jacket as she spoke, avoiding looking directly at him, paying more attention to buttoning it up than she needed to. "I can't do this anymore. I'm so, so sorry, but I can't." When she finally looked up at him, he saw regret in her eyes. He was sure she saw the same in his.

"I'm not surprised. I've been wearing you out with what I've needed from you," he said. He reached for her hand, but she didn't respond to his gesture.

"I've been only too happy to help. I love you. You know I do. But I'm…"

"Done with it?"

"I'd stay if I could. But this body of mine isn't what it used to be. I'm seventy. I need to have my hip replaced. I can't take care of two active boys while I'm in the hospital and at PT appointments."

"You don't need to apologize. I understand. You've been the best grandmother and mother-in-law anyone could ask for. I don't know what the boys and I would have done without you after Paula died."

Tears appeared at the mention of the death of her daughter—Jack's wife—from ovarian cancer two and a half years ago. "I wanted to help. Had to help or I'd have gone crazy. I hate to leave you in the lurch like this, but the doc says I shouldn't put it off any longer."

Jack hugged her. "We'll be fine. I'll start looking tomorrow for someone to help. When's the surgery?"

"Not for a month, so you have a little time." She patted her son-in-law on the arm. "I'm not sure what I'll miss the most—feeling like I'm helping you out or being a part of my grandsons' lives."

"You make it sound like you're moving to Timbuktu. You'll still be part of their lives."

"But not every day the way I've been since ... well, for the past couple years."

Anxious to assure her she wouldn't be losing touch with her grandsons, Jack said, "When you're back on your feet, we'll work something out so you see them regularly. Don't worry about it. Get yourself taken care of."

Anne gathered up her purse and several containers, now empty of the food she'd brought over to feed the three Richardson males. "Shall I tell the boys, or do you want to?"

"How about we both do it? When I've got someone else lined up, we'll tell them together. Fair enough?"

"More than fair." She put her arms around his waist in a farewell hug. "I wish I didn't have to do this."

"We can't have you working so hard you end up on the DL. Don would shoot me." Don was Anne's husband, the kids' grandfather.

"He wouldn't shoot you, although he might make your life a living hell at family dinners." She gave him a kiss on his cheek and released him. "You've looked out for everyone else for so long you haven't had a chance to do anything for yourself. And now I've made it even harder for you."

"You haven't. I'll be fine." Jack accompanied her to the door then watched her walk slowly to her car. The limp he'd begun to notice a few months back was more pronounced. Either it was worse or she was no longer trying to hide the pain. Whichever it was, it was why he hadn't been surprised at her announcement.

He was glad she was getting her hip taken care of, but he had to admit it did make his life more complicated. It was spring. The wheat on his Eastern Oregon ranch was beginning to produce heads of grain and needed attention. He had to get the rest of the alfalfa he'd use to feed his small herd of cattle over the winter planted. The same herd of cattle that had begun calving. Then there was the foal due from the mare his late wife had loved.

Now he had to add finding someone to help with kid wrangling. At the rate things were going, he'd be an old, old man before he'd have a chance to do what Anne suggested—find time for himself.

• • •

"Any extra shifts for me this week?" Quanna Morales asked her supervisor. "I'll even work a double."

"Sorry, kiddo, but unless someone calls in sick, I've got all the slots filled. Will you be around if I need you at the last minute?"

"I'm working the breakfast and lunch shift at the resort this weekend, but I'm available otherwise. You know how to find me."

"Believe me, if I need you, I'll find you. You're the most dependable part-timer on staff."

Her shift as an aide at the Golden Years Retirement Community over, Quanna headed for home with nothing to do for the rest of the day except fret about money. And how, if she didn't make more soon, she'd have to move back to the Umatilla Reservation where she'd grown up.

When she'd left for Portland so she could follow her dream of being a teacher, she had assumed that by the time she was in her late twenties, she'd be back on the rez in another way—teaching kids who needed to see that they, too, could have their dreams come true. But her life had unfolded a little differently than she had planned. The cost of living in the city and paying tuition was more than she'd imagined, so she'd had to recalculate how long it would take to get her degree. Then, about three years ago, her father died of a sudden heart attack, leaving her mother with few resources to take care of Miguel, her brother who'd been born with Down syndrome and several heart problems. She and her siblings had to pitch in. Quanna was the only unmarried one. So she volunteered to move back over the mountains to help financially and to be available to stay with her brother to give her mother some respite.

The two part-time jobs she'd patched together since coming back—her job at the retirement home as well as a shift every now and then at the restaurant in the resort on the rez—made it almost possible to afford her tiny apartment, a class at the local community college, and her contribution to her brother's care. The operative word being "almost." If something didn't change, she would have to move back in with her mother if she had any shot at achieving her goal of finishing her degree so she could teach.

With everything on her mind, the sunny day and the sweet, sage-y smells of spring in the high plains didn't lift her spirits the way they usually did. She was merely reminded by what was around her that another season had arrived with little progress toward her goals.

• • •

"I was glad to see you were working today," Quanna's friend Rita said when Quanna got to work in the middle of the following week. "I was afraid you'd miss out on the hot cowboy's usual visit to Joan Anthony." Rita was almost drooling as she glanced up and down the hall.

Of course Quanna knew who Rita meant. Every woman in the place knew the guy. Mrs. Anthony had once described him as a nephew who was more like a son. Most of the female staff described him as yummy.

He was older, probably in his mid-forties, and he was a real deal cowboy, not the "big hat, no cattle" kind. His boots were made for work not show, and for the clincher, he sported a Stetson tan in the summer—pale forehead, where his hat rode low, the rest of his face dark from the sun. His jeans, which fit like they'd been tailored for him, were what the staff appreciated most. Well, his tight Wrangler butt the jeans showed off.

His sandy brown hair always looked a little shaggy, and his deep chocolate eyes looked sad until he smiled and crinkles appeared around them to complement the dimples in his cheeks. He looked like he was in great shape and walked with the assurance of a man who was comfortable in his skin.

But there was something a little mysterious in the expression on his face, like he was holding something back. It was sexy and made all the women who drooled over him want to comfort him. Or something.

During his visits to Joan Anthony, some of the aides had been known to "drop by" her apartment to she if she needed anything just to get into a conversation with him. He was charming and funny, and they hoped by talking to him, they could uncover his secret, whatever it was. Quanna hadn't resorted to such an extreme. But she had asked Mrs. Anthony about him.

His name was Jack Richardson, and he ran a wheat operation twenty-five miles outside Pendleton. His late father was Mrs. Anthony's brother.

Today, however, instead of going directly to his aunt's apartment, Richardson went to the director's office. The staff gossip was hot and heavy about whether this meant Mrs. Anthony was about to be moved out of the facility or, if she stayed, transferred from independent to assisted living. She had, after all, been showing signs of slowing down recently, beginning to have trouble with some of the activities of daily living. Maybe her family had decided it was time to upgrade her level of care. The women all hoped she would be staying. She was one of the nicest people they cared for, and they would miss her. Not to mention miss seeing the hot cowboy.

Turned out, what he was apparently doing was asking permission to put a flier on the staff bulletin board before he went to see his aunt. Curious, Quanna took a look at what he posted the first chance she could. It was an advertisement for a job at the Richardson ranch, a "kid wrangler," as it was described, for two young boys, with additional light housekeeping and cooking duties. The job was full time. The pay worked out to be double the hourly rate she was making at the retirement facility. Although she had no childcare experience other than babysitting when she was a teenager, Quanna was sure she could craft her résumé to show she had the skills needed. This could be the answer to her money problems. If only there were some way to ensure she had the inside track for the job.

Maybe there was. At the bottom of the flier were tear-off bits of paper with a phone number and e-mail address on each piece. Looking around to make sure no one was watching, she carefully tore off all but two of the pieces. She wanted the job. If it took cheating to get it, she was willing to do it.

Instead of going home at the end of her shift that day, Quanna waited in the parking lot for the cowboy to appear. Feeling like she was stalking him—because, face it, she was—she followed him and watched where he posted more fliers. When he headed out of town, she returned to each place and removed most of the tear-off tags from the fliers. She didn't think it was smart to remove them all. He'd think it odd if she was the only person who contacted him about the job.

But she would make sure she was one of only a handful. That would lower the odds of someone more qualified getting the job she already thought of as hers. At least, she hoped it would.

Praise for *Thankful for Love*:

"Ms. Bird isn't afraid to add flavor to her piece by using unconventional characters … This is a beautifully written novel that makes the reader feel good for having gotten to know the characters." —**InD'Tale Magazine**

For more from Peggy Bird, check out:

A Holiday for Love series:

Sparked by Love

Praise for *Sparked by Love*:

"With lies and hidden agendas, you have to wait and see till the very end for all the pieces to fall together!" —Chicks That Read

"A warm, fuzzy romance read. Leo and Shannon are just so sweet together. There is plenty of steam as well. Very enjoyable read for romance lovers." —Wilovebooks, 4 stars

"This book had the Triple 'S' factor for me: short, sweet and sexy … a wonderful book." —Red's Hot Reads, 4 stars

"This was my first time reading Peggy Bird. I was pleasantly surprised by not only her writing style, which was very engaging and flowed, but also her characters." —Book Nerd, 4 stars

Unmasking Love

Praise for *Unmasking Love:*

"Spicy and modernized, this story relies on the mystique and romance of Romeo and Juliet, without the bad ending. Peggy Bird brings heat and heart to Halloween." —4 stars, I Am, Indeed

"I love the author's witty writing style, which is present right from the opening lines of this book. Ms. Bird successfully builds deliciously, believable sexual tension between Julie and Trace; you can almost hear the cracks of electricity!"—5 stars, Ellesea Loves Reading

"The story isn't long, but it wasn't rushed. ... Beautifully written and wonderfully engaging."—4 stars, Written Love Reviews

Lights, Latkes, and Love

Ringing in Love

The Gift of Love

Second Chances series:

Beginning Again

Praise for *Beginning Again*:

"Both Liz and Collins are great characters. Liz is not a bitter middle aged woman, but instead a very strong and brave lady. I really enjoyed *Beginning Again* because it was an easy read that made my gray autumn day a little bit less gray." —Long & Short Reviews

Loving Again

Together Again

Praise for *Together Again*:

"...a very enjoyable romance. I loved the main characters and the great writing. I always admire strong, independent women, so if you also enjoy those qualities in a heroine, and enjoy a well-written romance, I recommend this one." —Night Owl Reviews

Trusting Again

Praise for *Trusting Again*:

"The book moves along at a nice pace and the characters are believable and realistic. It is a well-written story with a wonderful ending!" —Harlequin Junkie

Believing Again

Falling Again

In the mood for more Crimson Romance?
Check out *What the Bachelor Gets by Kristina Knight* at
CrimsonRomance.com.

www.ingramcontent.com/pod-product-compliance
Lightning Source LLC
Chambersburg PA
CBHW010311100726
47905CB00011B/3289